GW01605258

BOYCHESTER'S BUGLE

Alan Franks

NEW ENGLISH LIBRARY

First published in Great Britain in 1982 by William Heinemann Ltd

First NEL Paperback Edition September 1983

NEL Books are published by
New English Library,
Mill Road, Dunton Green,
Sevenoaks, Kent.
Editorial office: 47 Bedford Square, London WC1B 3DP

Printed and bound in Great Britain by
Cox & Wyman Ltd, Reading

British Library C.I.P.

Franks, Alan
Boychester's bugle.
I. Title
823'.914[F]   PR6057.R/

ISBN 0-450-05627-9

Contents

I	The Coming Men	1
II	Partitions	20
III	Conversions	36
IV	Inspections	80
V	Last Orders	106
VI	The Final Issue	137

For
Susan

I
The Coming Men

"THE METAL BEAST," said Boychester as gravely as he could, "has taken in a peach and blown out a raspberry."

As always on these occasions the line was heavy with rehearsing. He looked around the newsroom at his captive audience to spread the guilt of the day. Only Mrs. Weekes was looking back at him with a nod at the ready. The other four remained in mock contrition, heads down, in the dusty shafts of sunlight that broadened in from the window.

"A raspberry," he said again, giving the *Bugle* another petulant slap. He was framed in the brightness of the window, barely more than a silhouette to the onlookers. This too was planned. Behind him in the memorial garden the noises of the July morning fell away as he turned the handle that closed the top flap.

In the middle of the group was David Camina. Behind lenses as thick as wine bottles was the heavily Jewish "Y" of eyebrows and nose. It was a face that would have looked at home on any Prisoner of Conscience poster. Even the bone structure seemed to have been made with emaciation in mind. He shot a glance up at Boychester's outline. The editor's voice was rising with pique, but to Camina it was growing as blurred as the man's image. He could make out the shape of the sow-suit, so called because of the showy rows of buttons that ran in columns down the waistcoat like vestigial teats. The jacket was padded square to hide shoulders which sloped naturally from neck to arm on a one in three gradient. There was not a ripple of movement as the cigarette was raised mouthwards.

It seemed to Camina at that moment that his lot and Boychester's must have been ordained an eternity ago; that they had been meeting across history in essentially similar contexts – always Boychester with the whip hand, Boychester crossed, Boychester pouting, seeking redress, and Camina forever stateless and awkward, his very existence a matter of debate.

"A ruddy raspberry," the voice said again. To seasoned Boychester watchers there was no mistaking the signs. "Ruddy" meant: "See. I am driven to strong language, but mark with what restraint."

Boychester was fat in a style that only the English male has mastered. Almost all the excess weight was in a girdle of flesh at waist height. It was worth at least four stone and there was no shifting it. It went all the way round and made the trunk look like a bell, tapering up to the chest and shoulders. Somehow the thighs hadn't responded to the challenge. They were still thin and unmuscled. Even when he shifted his stance the trousers hardly changed shape. They just shook a little, like a curtain flicked from behind.

Cathal Dwyer, standing between Camina and Mrs. Weekes, was next to glance up towards the window. He prickled with longing for a drink, and the image he took back from the glare was one of nothing but circles. There was the round face of the clock on the wall, brisk and uncompromising when the deadlines neared, but mercilessly slow this morning; there was the circular shape of

Boychester's head. It glistened with the orange pigment that always found its way into his hair and skin when he was agitated. There were the two rims of his schoolboy spectacles. On his lapel was the smallest circle, a tiny golden wheel with a knurled rim. It was a Rotary Club badge and it shone keenly as a beacon of his new allegiances.

Cathal found it revolting. Things would be better in the Two Chairmen, the pub that shared the island site with the printing works and memorial garden. He would walk in (it was past opening time already), and Maire, without a word, would push the optic up with a glass, wait for the bubbles, then push again for the second measure. It all happened as silently as prayer. Logic and patience were evasive until that time.

There could hardly have been a bigger contrast between the looks of the two men. Cathal, for all the years of excess, still had a fine, lean face even if its very best days, like so much about him, belonged in history. He was tall as the poplar, mournful as the willow, and he was a County Clare man. His skin was still florid with the Iberian blood that had sailed north to stiffen a wavering Catholica Fide all those centuries before. He was born part eagle and part terrier, and the two creatures were always at odds; his 60 years had been lived somewhere between noble flight and a scrap on the pavement.

There was a mounting hysteria about Boychester since his elevation, and since the knowledge that the days of the metal beast, the absurd dying metabolism that clanked beyond the partition, were numbered. Control was at the heart of the matter, thought Cathal. Control and ownership. Not ownership of the building or the presses, or anything as tangible as that, but of all the scraps of rumour and half-knowledge that had started to litter the place recently.

Boychester sought them out like a Hoover. Nature had made him deeply indifferent to his fellow man and this inquiring role was a new one that sat awkwardly on him.

Besides, things had started galloping of late. Events were getting a momentum of their own and Boychester was locked to them grimly, like a novice on a bolting pony. It had all started with the Holborn declaration about new technology. The decree from head office, where all the other five titles were based, had carried the ring of Empire; the rusting ingenuities of Gutenburg were soon for the breakers' yard. In their place would come those quiet and germless screens where sentences marshalled themselves unaided. It concentrated the mind alarmingly. The building too was probably to be condemned, and the pub. No-one would just sit on such a site like they used to in the early seventies. In time everything would go. The whiff of change and rationalisation was abroad. This outpost of the *Bugle* would have to give an account of itself. It was as if some thrusting junior in the Foreign Office had suddenly lighted on Belize; and here was Boychester, the fly-blown governor, hastily looking to his plumage.

Everything was in flux now, everything up for grabs. Cathal owned few impulses beyond pure survival, and the new tempo was offensive. He thought of moles that spread to signal the onset of cancer, of cells caught up in a rude reshuffle.

Naturally Boychester's push for omniscience stopped short of taking the blame for errors like today's. Which is why he was now trying, in the vaguest of terms, to taint his minions with the shame of that colossal misprint. It squatted like a tramp in the text of his leader, beyond explanation and far beyond quoting. It was simply there, defiantly and with no respect.

The "peach" he referred to was his line on council spending. This was the usual mixture of fawning, hectoring and sheer plagiarism. Except that today it was shot through with foreign bodies of every kind, fractions and blobs and asterisks, all spilled down at random in the type. In places it looked like a series of half-formed obscenities spat out by someone with a terrible defect. Boychester trying to salvage some dignity from the mess was the purest mock-heroic. It would have been funnier if it had not been an exercise in blame-sharing. As it was, everyone knew he had been with one of the Buyers the previous evening, when he should have been checking the last pages.

A word about the Buyers. There must have been a hard core of about six, all with names like Ffitch and Pimlott. What they bought was food and drink for Boychester, and through it immunity for their masters from a bad press. They were PR men, and their stock-in-trade was information withheld. They loved Boychester's company and the feeling was mutual. You could see them at three-ish in Domingo's, as moist and rosy as their guest from the leaking of false confidences. Often the editor couldn't even remember where they came from. But it hardly mattered. For those two magic hours Boychester and Buyer would sit back and look at each other across the table, as if at a mirror, astounding themselves with the beauty of their own performance. Sometimes, after particularly good lunches, there was no talking at all, just coded Mmms and Yahs, and folded slips of paper with a cash figure being passed across. Nothing ever found its way into print. That would have been a violation. This was power without responsibility, and Stanley Baldwin's harlot never enjoyed her prerogative more richly.

It was with Ffitch that Boychester had been the previous

evening while printers had come and gone from the newsroom, cursing him in his absence and eventually running the page uncorrected.

Cathal heard the voice rise again as it came to the end of the harangue. He heard the name of Sizer mentioned, the appalling systems expert freshly installed at Holborn to usher in the new technology. Sizer, he remembered, was the one who looked like a television and spoke in the grotesque new parlance of the coming man. He was the one whom Boychester had been courting mightily, desperate for a private alliance. He was one of nature's filing clerks, puffed up to an importance that only a technocrat could enjoy these days. Suddenly the world was full of them.

"Clearly," said Boychester, "I cannot promise that head office will not view . . . this with dismay." Another slap of the *Bugle*. Mrs. Weekes prepared another receptive nod and Pam and Harvey, the colleague-lovers at the end of the row, shifted on their feet.

At last, with a stagey flourish, Boychester laid the guilty paper on the table and strode for the door. The clanking grew louder as he passed through. The taste of the man cleared from Cathal's palate, and he thought again of Maire at the optic. Somehow Boychester always had a taste these days. It was hard to describe, but there was an orange flavour about his presence, like the colour that fingered its way over his flesh. He had become permeating. No-one felt it more strongly than Cathal, which was understandable. Boychester smelled subversion here. He wanted to own the contents of the Irishman's head, to have his thoughts and to forage in him for as long as it took to get at them. Already he had started the Saturday morning searches of Cathal's desk, when there was no-one about, and he did not like what he had found. Even so, it would have been hard to guess at that stage the lengths to which his loathing was to run – the raising of an indiscretion to a capital offence, the whole court case business with the nuns, and the paper's weird role as England's gallows tree.

Boychester moved through the works like an ill wind. There were little stirrings as he passed, little nudges and whispers. He could feel himself causing the activity.

On the left in a recess a young West Indian was carding impurities from a trough of molten lead, occasionally wiping the card off between his fingers. He looked up scornfully from his work.

The compositors were standing in line at the stone, the long metal table where the pages were put together. They wore felt aprons which dented at the midriff as they leaned over to deal type into the frames. Many times in the past, particularly after a good issue, Boychester had managed a swarm of affection for these men. He had seen them as porters handling the physical weight of his prose; or as postmen delivering his personal message to the borough. Today they looked arch and mutinous. The wrists that lifted the trays were crude and sinewy. They were a bunch of ruddy inkies.

Further down the works were the linotype operators, in an area cased by glass. They sat in two rows, each man at a machine that could have been a typewriter dreamed up in madness. Behind the keyboard was a jungle of metal, and at the side polished wheels and bands. Every few seconds a long steel arm rose nearly vertically and there was a clatter of lead slugs down a chute. Machine and man seemed grey with obsolescence. The two rows had the look of a coxless eight in disarray.

"Absurd regatta," Boychester muttered as he passed. To him the very term "hot metal" suddenly belonged to antiquity, the worthy age of Telford and Brunel. Mr. Sizer would agree.

He carried on through the rubber doors and down a spiral into the bowels of the beast. More men in overalls were sitting near the press, reading the racing pages and sipping tea. On the wall behind them was a yellowing copy of an old Factories Act, with clauses ringed in red.

The presses were quiet at the moment. But it was a room made for noise and even this partial silence had a way of stopping talk. Over by a belt of revolving spindles were piles of the *Bugle*, next to some of the other titles. Boychester felt the heat of more smirks in his direction. He walked into the bright sunlight of the loading bay, and out into Fountain Street. On a bench in the memorial garden a tramp was sitting with his head between his knees over a bottle of cider. His suede shoes had turned shiny, and Boychester tutted with disgust. Mendicancy would be the topic of his next leader.

Outside the Two Chairmen he hailed a taxi and made for Holborn. As they stopped and started between the traffic lights of the Harrow Road, he dipped into his pockets for the tattered pieces of paper with Cathal's handwriting. They were the fruits of his latest trawl in the Irishman's drawer, and some had almost turned to pap. He could still not make out most of the writing. It was set out like a play, with two characters' names recurring down the margin. Some words were in a foreign script. The sheet which he kept returning to had written on the bottom:

"N. B. B'ch'st as model of Brit. oppression." This was clearly stamped in capitals as a memo to an author aware of his own forgetfulness. The other lines were full of exclamation marks, as though the characters were locked in fierce argument.

The taxi reached Holborn and Boychester stuffed the pieces back in his pocket. He walked across the main road, then down the alley next to Staples Inn Buildings. This was far more his kind of area, particularly since the declaration. It was heavy and sober with litigation, and not a place to be pushed around, lightly altered or left to rot. It not only knew all the rules, it created some of them, either by precedent or practice. It was as Boychester would have liked to be himself. Even the half-timbered buildings that had been pressed out of true by the years had the eccentricities of the basically solid character. In his mind's eye he had his own name substituted for the ones on the solicitors' plaques that he passed, but with the suffixes of initials kept intact.

Lunch with Sizer was not a triumph. The two met in the dark eating area at the back of a pub filled with lawyers. The place was teeming with wise saws and modern instances, chapter and verse. There were cocky young clerks who now knew that their life's delight was to see grown men laid low by due process of law, to be the conductors of all that voltage.

Boychester was tacky around the neck and in his palms. He sat facing Sizer across a table for two, just as he would with a Buyer. But it was a very different experience. At about the stage when he would normally expect to feel a surge of importance rising in him, he felt very vulnerable. Sizer, with his jargon of "game plan", "scenario" and "downside" was playing at home.

He was saying: "Strikes me your *Bugle*'ll be staffed in-house come cold type."

Boychester said "yes" blankly.

"No other way, eh? Course, there'll be a bit of fat-trimming, goes without saying. Union chappie, are you?"

Boychester went moister still and prepared a withering dismissal of the union. But Sizer cut him short with "No, sorry. None of my business."

His face puckered with contempt and he went on: "You know, Boychester, some of those inkies up your way think the world owes them a living. Ridiculous."

"Ridiculous, sir."

"I mean, they really believe that they can hold up newtech for ever. And look at the old gear they've got up there. They wouldn't touch it if it was a used car."

"Certainly not."

"Apart from anything else, no-one's making the parts any more. They're all packing up. You can't get them for love nor money. Every other country in the world knows that – except us. What you've got up there is an utter lash-up."

Boychester sensed a wildness emitting from the coming man. There was a glint in his eye as sharp as the Rotary badge which he too had on his lapel. It was the look of a fanatic.

"Look, the board's four square behind me on this one," he continued. "Particularly the old man. He's seen those damn'd pinkos off before and he'll do it again, you mark my words."

The pub was clearing as the lawyers went briskly back to work. Sizer calmed a little and leaned forward confidentially. "I've seen systems, Boychester," he said. "Believe you me, I've seen systems. And the one we've lined up with Compucomp is a cracking good one. It's a belter."

"I'm sure."

"As far as your lot's concerned, I see it panning out as follows." He shifted an ash-tray to the centre of the table. "Here's Holborn, right? Now then, come newtech, what've we got? Correct. Bags of capacity. Absolutely bags of the stuff. And up here at your end?" He picked up a sugar bowl from the edge. "Right again. A vacuum. So what happens?"

Boychester winced as the sugar bowl was lifted over to the ash-tray, his own domain in this pudgy vice.

"An elision situation," said Sizer. "An elision situation if ever there was one."

With the triumph of someone proving his case beyond dissent, Sizer beckoned the waiter and paid the bill.

Outside in the brightness they parted, and Boychester soon found himself back in High Holborn. He was standing opposite an empty site that had laid the side of a large insurance building open to view. The temple-like frontage looked suddenly absurd now that the humdrum brickwork at the back was exposed, with its mean windows and its rows of pipes that gave away the position of the toilets.

He thought of that phrase of Sizer's – fat-trimming – and hardened his resolve to chest whatever cards he might have. Any impulse – and there had been the glimmer of one – to project himself as the champion of his little staff was stillborn and incinerated. If an angry sea was going to boil around the island site in Kilburn, they would have to find their own lifeboats. It was bad enough to have to seek the good opinion of a man like Sizer, but the alternatives were unthinkable; to take orders from people barely more than half his age. Boychester do this, Boychester do that, not good enough, Boychester. That way madness lay.

There was a stop in the mind. Besides, he owed Cathal and the others no favours. On the contrary. As for Camina, what a mistake that had been. Fancy thinking he had been buying into class with that appointment. The boy was too private and subversive by half.

Boychester looked at his watch and decided not to go back to work for the afternoon. There would only be more calls from furious readers and advertisers about the errors. The others could deal with them. He strolled up towards Clerkenwell. Every other building here seemed to house a little printing shop. They were of all kinds – old and new, converted homes, garages, warehouses, all with white-lit interiors and boys running to and fro with messages. This had been a seedbed of the Radicals' journals. Even today, with its one-way streets and secretive passages, it would have been a good enough setting for a war of the Unstamped Press. The thought even occurred to Boychester, but he felt uncomfortable with the heroic precedents of his trade, and was quickly back in his own worries.

Another taxi, this time home to Brondesbury. Another scrutiny of Cathal's writing. He could just about make out one of the names in the margin as being Flaherty. The character seemed to be at the peak of a rant. To judge from the commas, he was reeling off a list, of which the only recognisable things were Wexford and Drogheda, made bold by repeated pencil strokes. Then the page ended. Tomorrow was Saturday, and perhaps there would be more in the drawer by then.

It was a resented fact that Boychester had married well; well enough to snatch him several rungs up the social ladder. Certainly he was well clear of the filthy rack-renting bog in which Cathal, Camina and a million more still foundered. Almost overnight the urban decay that had filled his leaders once had become an unfashionable outrage. More than that, it had become the fault of its own victims. Take the last word of this morning's leader on the subject, somehow left unmauled by the metal beast: "God helps those who help themselves." The notion stood at the confluence of High Conservatism and civic Christianity, both subscribed to with the ardour of the new recruit.

Mrs. Boychester was a huge red-haired woman, rinsed pink and blameless by an only childhood in Surrey. If ever a wife went undeserved it was she. Her parents had given the world a blank page, ready for the imprint of any ideology. Boychester was not quite what they had had in mind, but then this great glowing bait did seem to be getting shouldered aside by all the other male fish in the river.

Boychester had taken speedily to the whole set-up. He had even started to use the strange *patois* of his mother-in-law, putting the sound of "agger" on the end of words, so that holiday would become holidagger, caravan caravagger and so on. Apparently this was the result of colonial parentage and a history of public schooling in the boys of her family. Wherever it came from, it sounded ridiculous from Boychester, who took it to be a stamp of breeding.

The father-in-law was a stockbroker who liked to disparage his home acres as "Green Line country, but good enough, I suppose." It was definitely good enough for Boychester, for whom it was the habitat of a new peer group.

Mrs. Boychester had produced an owlish and perplexed little boy, now three, called George, a replica of his father. It was one of philology's mysteries that his name had been visited with the "o" mutation, making him Jogger. He would fall silent whenever his father appeared, and brace himself for some bizarre adult gambit.

For the second time today Boychester, immersed in his reading, was surprised to be at his destination already. He paid the driver and climbed the front steps of his house. Those days he referred to it – but only half as a joke – as Boychester Towers. It started because of Larch Towers, the prep school across the road, which acquired a new wing or art room every time you turned your back. It had made Boychester feel competitive. As with a face that's pulled, the wind had changed and the joke had stuck.

The front door opened and George scampered from view. Mrs. Boychester stood there in her usual pose, arms spread wide to lift an acreage of loose dress. She was so guileless that she believed the *Bugle*'s misprints to be the typing errors of her husband's secretary. Boychester was not about to disabuse her. As he reached the top step his orange head disappeared in her embrace and she gave the usual greeting: "Clever Boychy!" It was always Clever Boychy. Not for anything in particular. Just for being.

That lunch-time the Two Chairmen was Cathal's oyster. Maire performed like clockwork as she saw him enter. She could have been an expensive toy activated by a trip switch on the threshold. As the whisky went down he loosened and grew, and shuffled off the dead skin of the morning. Soon the little bar was full. Even Mrs. Weekes was there, and Pam and Harvey.

"Boychester," Cathal announced at length, "is no cathedral."

It went unchallenged.

"And why is he no cathedral? I shall tell you. A good cathedral – take whichever you will – soars."

His arm pointed up at the ceiling.

"Gravity is of no consequence to the stones. They go up, up, up. Now, you may well wonder what the hell they think they're about, but up they still go."

He had an audience. Mick, the landlord, had heard his favourite customer in full flow and had come out from the back. He had a bruise of a nose and cheeks tattooed with spidery veins from years of free stock.

"Boychester, on the other hand," Cathal continued, "goes that-a-way." The same arm was stabbing down towards the floor, as if putting a sick dog out of its misery. "Everything down. Jowls down, shoulders down, paps down, paunch down. Down, down, down. The man has a Hellward thrust and the Devil is not happy about it."

Mick brought a poteen bottle from under the counter and poured measures for Cathal and himself. There was no greater honour than this, particularly with police using the pub these days. The bottle was put away again and none of the others at the bar felt excluded.

"So Cathal," said Mick, "there are changes in the wind, yes?"

"Changes, yes. Funny screens and things. Whole place'll go."

"Ah well. And your man Barchester is crowing on the dung pile, I expect?"

"He has his tongue up the TV man's arse, yes."

Mrs. Weekes blushed and left for court. The afternoon would yield up another little harvest of retribution and swell her stacks of brick-coloured copy paper on the office shelves – "my Pinkies," as she called them; "my guilty ones."

Mick drained his glass and in the same movement reached down for the bottle again.

"What'll we drink to now, Cathal?" he said. "There's always something to drink to. What about the TV man?"

"Why the TV man? Honestly, he's not worth it, Mick."

"I'm thinking that what with Barchester having a forked tongue, it must be a little, you know, painful for him."

"Oh, he doesn't need to be drunk to," said Cathal. "Not him nor Boychester. They're the coming men. Also, Mick, they have the art of the day."

He put on a look of mystery, like someone telling a child a ghost story. Maire leant her chin on her hand, puzzled again.

"The art of the present," said Cathal.

"And what is that?" asked the landlord.

"It's all a question of middle fingers, Mick. A question of whether you can stab and mutter."

"Is that right?"

"Pocket calculators, you know. Everyone today has a thing about little shifting figures behind glass. If you can only make the right row come up, then you're king of the pile. So it's stab and mutter, stab and mutter, see? Why, there's dozens of men doing it in their offices all day long."

"There's a thing," said Mick. "So will we drink to the right row coming up?"

"Not so fast. Right row for them means wrong row for us. That's usually the way."

"Wrong row, right row," said Mick. "We'll drink in any event. That woman . . ."

"Mrs. Weekes?"

"The one who just flounced out, yes. Is she one of you? I've my doubts somehow. Can we drink to her?"

"She's one of her own, and a bit of the beak's. Loves nothing more than a case that goes hard for the defendant. When she gets back you can nearly tell the size of the fine by the spread of her grin."

"That's a most peculiar game, Cathal, that court covering. Like sneaking, sort of. You know, listening all attentive, and then, well, blurting."

"There's some come up who shouldn't be there at all, and others never up who should be."

"And Mrs. Weekes is always there then, Cathal?"

"Never misses a show. It's the odd little ones she goes for. Flashers and I don't know what."

"And your man Barchester. What does he say to that?"

"Boychester? Oh my word. He lets it run."

Maire swivelled her head back to Mick and said: "It sounds kinky to me."

"Well, dear," said Cathal, "our Mrs. Weekes has seen dark days."

The mystery came over his face again and he leant confidingly across the bar. "You see, her husband was killed by a lavatory."

"Get away, Cathal," said Maire.

"A lavatory," he repeated. He was suppressing a laugh with difficulty. "The poor man was *in situ*. He pulled the chain and the cistern fell on him. She found him there, with the pipes all bent off from the wall, and water everywhere. Killed instantly, the coroner said. Still, a terrible way for a man to go."

"Oh that's ghastly, Mick," said Maire, open-mouthed.

"And Mrs. Weekes has been, well, getting her own back. Courts and inquests. Inquests and courts. She can't have enough of it. Set her on a hard bench with a good charge sheet in her hand and she's as happy as Larry."

"I think we won't drink to her, Cathal," said Mick.

"If there's any folly about, she'll have it for herself," said Cathal.

"And it would be folly to waste good spirits on a woman like that."

In a few minutes Maire was ducking under the bar and shouting "Boys and girls, now please" at the top of her voice. She was scurrying round the little room like a mad girl in a farmyard, lifting up half-empty glasses to flick her cloth across the tables. Almost at once the place emptied itself into Fountain Street.

Mick looked down at the last quarter of the bottle and said to Cathal, more as a statement than a question: "You're staying."

Maire stood on a stool at the door to push the bolt home and the pub was quiet. Already Cathal felt the melancholy falling on him that seemed to follow all activity these days, making it seem meaningless. The poteen had taken its toll.

During the afternoon there were two or three muffled knocks at the door in the side alley, and Mick went through to open it. First there was a big man in the casual clothes that always betray an off-duty policeman. Later there was one of Mick's Republican friends, the one who came round on Saturday nights with a collection box, and Cathal wondered hazily at the contrast of the visitors.

Very soon the doors re-opened and the bar was crowded again. The time seemed to stand still and to fly, all at once. He tried to prepare his Clearances speech, the one that likened Sizer's campaign to the purging of the Highlands, but it kept running away from him. The future seemed grey and usurious, and there was a kind of solace to be had from the past, however bloody. It would come, it would come.

Meanwhile, up in the magistrate's court Mrs. Weekes feigned piety as the same old felons were fed again through the shame machine.

II
Partitions

THE NEXT DAY, a Saturday, the first dew of the morning was breaking over Cathal in his bed. It was going to be another boiling day, and already the light was aching its way through the flimsy curtain. It caught the sharp nose that was just breaking surface from under the sheet, and the long white fingers on the end of an arm that hung out from the bed as if to say: "Welcome. This is it."

Beyond the hand was the pile of clothes that Cathal had stamped out of last thing at night after another half-remembered session in the Chairmen. They squatted there like some animate thing just resting for a moment. The boots were splayed at right angles like Cathal's feet in mid-rant. The trousers must have dropped absolutely straight, as the toe-caps of the boots still stuck out in front of them. On top was the tweed jacket with the elbow patches that had slumped down after the shirt; somehow it had stayed in a rigid sort of triangle, helped by the letters, books, cuttings, flask and wallet which it housed. Last of all, round the neck of the jacket, was the little yellow crescent of the scarf, perfect as a smoke ring. The whole elevation of the pile was not more than twenty inches, a little headless dwarf waiting for his might to return.

Behind it was a rustling of straw in the half-light, then a fast series of metal pings. A quivering nose peered out through the bars and the eyes above it darkened in terror as they caught sight of the Cathal dwarf. Then there was a squeal, not from the creature but from the wheel which he had boarded and was operating at full tilt with his back hollowed and his front paws tearing away at eye level like a lion rampant. This was Charles Stewart Parnell, hamster, and he was sounding the alarm.

The alarm joined the light and mounted a second assault on Cathal's brain. His whole face was shut tight against the horrors of the day. Castle Cathal would not be stormed. The undersheet was cold and damp with sweat, and beneath that a slow dark patch was spreading in the worst-hit areas. Tiny rivers were picking up from their sources, then dropping in a globule down an arm or a thigh.

His feet flailed slightly and then all of a sudden his entire body seemed to rise three inches above the bed, whip over in the air on to its back and drop down again. Still the eyes were shut, but the light was sharpening around them. Convulsively he wiped his nose with a cross-blow from the back of his hand and muttered aloud to Maire, who was not with him: "Jesus girlie, we have shifted some barley tonight."

Maire; always the image of Maire it was that came to him at dire times like these, which were frequent. Last night had been a whopper, after the pub filled up again, and this was bad, very bad.

He mumbled again: "And a little one for Mrs. Weekes, yes?"

Maire never asked any questions, just gave him the things he wanted, mostly large ones.

"Mrs. Weekes," he murmured. "Oh she's gone, has she? That's good. We can let our hair down, what?"

Maire always gave him the answers he wanted too, even if they were mute ones. What a perfect relationship it was. This seemed to be the single lucid strand in a hot and scrambled head. A match based entirely on supply and demand in precise measure.

As for sex, nothing as troublesome as that muddied the pool. Perhaps an arm round her back at chucking-out, by which time every nerve of pain or pleasure within him would be too cauterised to feed any data from hand to groin. Physical love was for other people, and in other vessels. Sensuality was the touch of Maire's hand at the bottle-end, followed by the spurting of a sixth of a gill. There was nothing to approach that.

Gradually he came to. As he tried to fill in the gaps of the previous night, Parnell started the wheel again.

"Will you put a sock in it, sir!" He propped himself up on an elbow, opened his eyes, red as his room-mate's, and clenched a fist towards the cage. "Fine, so you've a metal beast of your own. If the damn'd thing is not stopped forthwith it will be hit by the new technology. Do you fancy the notion of spinning round and round on a Sizer screen? Well?"

Mr. Parnell didn't fancy it. He scrambled from the wheel and gestured wildly with his nose through the bars at the stranger on the carpet.

Cathal looked down at it also and said: "Bit crumpled today, Cathal Dwyer?"

Parnell looked back and forth between the two.

"And what were you up to last night, my fine little man, that you wake like a concertina? Ah, we're all hunchy and dumb insolent are we? Been on the juice is my guess. Look at the state of you. No head, for a start."

For some reason the jacket picked this moment to leave the debate, and toppled slowly on to its side.

"Most spineless. Need a stiffener, I expect. Can't start the day without me."

He swivelled off the bed and kicked the jacket in the back of its neck, which was still pointed. It hooked on to his foot and shot through the air, landing with a clang around the cage. Cathal fell back again on the bed. Last night, though he could not remember it, had been triumphant. He had swooped and cathedralled for two hours, railing against Boychester, Sizer and the new technology.

Now the glory had passed and he was back in the grip of depression, where he mostly lived. He had got used to the feel of failure round him like a cloak. It was a foul piece of clothing, but he gave it a certain style. Let someone run at him with patronage and he would swirl the attacker on into thin air.

But depression was inside as well as out, a conscientious cancer. He would have left it behind him at his last lodging, like a bag of stinking laundry that the next man must deal with. Except that these days it followed him around. What was there to show for all these years? A huge turnover of jobs in papers from Newcastle to Exeter, the names of which he couldn't even begin to remember, let alone the sequence. And each one of them accompanied by this same dismal cell. Different addresses but still basically the same room: a bed, a wardrobe, the suitcase on top, a cooker, latterly the cage, and on the other side of the door the same landing with bubbly lino and a permanent smell of gas; on the walls the same veinwork of pipes, wheezing and rattling with the turn of a tap somewhere in the building. Twenty years of going into offices which were getting younger by the day, in order to write the same story around different names: "Pensioner Bill Subberthwaite had a nasty surprise when he came home from a fortnight in Skegness. His house had gone."

Yet these particular pipes were original, he had to admit. Whenever Camina in the upstairs room played an E on his flute they rattled, and when they did the whole house shook like a jelly. "Don't give us an E now, Camina. Anything but an E this morning."

Before England what? Same sort of thing in Cork and the south. Then the final separation back in Kilrush, the guilt, the wretched and unremitting Catholic disdain, the leaving, and the beginning of this – the hate and love for the old country growing in tandem. The sow did indeed devour her own farrow.

He swung his legs off the bed, opened the door and padded naked down the stairs to the front door, outside which the papers would be waiting, his second sole extravagance. The newsboy in a hurry had left them not quite at the top of the concrete flight. Cathal opened the door ajar and tried to squeeze a shoulder and an arm across the mat and down the top step. He crawled forward, barging the door fully open behind him, and stretched full-length for the bundle. To the passers-by, who were two nuns, his whole body could be seen issuing from the house, ankles in the dark, backside hinging down on the top step, scrawny back and arms struggling for a hold on the papers. Stuck like this, he bobbed his head up and exclaimed: "Worm coming down pyramid. Morning, girls."

The nuns passed on without a word. Cathal ground himself back up the steps, slammed the front door and tottered back up to his room. Again he crashed down on to the bed to assess the week's callow views of the world, while Mr. Parnell heckled from his wheel.

"Tito's had it," he said. "Afghanistan is all to shit." He turned to the home pages of the *Guardian*, which were screaming of conditions in Parkhurst. "Got nothing on the Maze," he muttered. "Nothing at all."

He turned over to the arts, where there lurked brilliant young people with answers and beauty. "Can't move for genius," he said. Here a 24-year-old poet was smiling knowingly from his strip of adulation. There a first play-wright was "standing the received wisdom on its head." Martin de Crespigny's was "an unremittingly bleak vision into which the merest pin-prick of optimism is allowed to intrude as the nurse finally agrees to be seduced by Roland's Doberman."

"We're bristling with visions today, Mr. Parnell. Positively bristling. One thing we are not going to have to go short on in these straitened days is a vision."

In time, however, all these heads would bow at the passing of the masterpiece, Cathal's triumph. It was one of those rare works that was a classic even before it was completed, to the extent that it could be all the things it had to be without being fully written. It was called "The Partition," and used most brilliantly the analogy of a divided pub, The Erin, for the establishment of the border between Eire and Ulster. So perfect was the conceit that everything – the old ascendancy, the religious ratios in the population, the shifting of the electoral boundaries (there was even a floating drinker called Gerry Mander), yes, and the American dimension; all these things and more could be encompassed. Some customers wanted to stay with the British brewery. Others favoured a free house. The tenant, his wife and children, each lobbied for their own factions, and so on until the arrival of the Special Patrol Group for the protection of the customers as Last Orders ("Yeats' fifth bell") approached.

If a literary historian had had the presence of mind to be in this room he would have been able to lay his hands on the earliest fragments of The Partition. The main archive was the tweed jacket. It had so many pockets that the search could have been a long one. The clearest passage had been worn into the right inside breast pocket, but there were other rents in the lining each opening on to its own treasure.

With the long habits of a survivor he would often divide his wages each week and put different bits into different pockets. It was a sort of reserve tank system, except that it didn't work because he knew it was there all the time and as often as not plundered it deeply on the very night of pay day, clawing out pieces of the dialogue together with pound notes. And Maire would say: "Sorry Connell, but it's not legal tender."

Quite a lot of The Partition, including possibly the most precious piece, Flaherty's monologue, had gone down through the lining and was lost in the dark. Sometimes in the Chairmen Cathal would stand up, keel from the waist until the panel hung, then tap the weight with his hand as you might a flak jacket. "Are you within, Flaherty?" he would enquire, and then sit down satisfied. At later hours in the lavatory in the back alley bits of Flaherty might be taken out and declaimed to the wall.

There was of course also the nearly finished argument scene, still in Cathal's drawer at work, which would have to be dovetailed with the rest.

He stood up and started to dress from the pile, stooping

creakily for each garment, and thinking about Boychester. He had said some triumphant things on that subject again last night, if he could only get them back.

He had always sworn that a note taken in drink would only become decipherable again after a good top-up the next day. In fact he had lived much of his life on that principle. If only the same held true of the things he said. For example, had the Clearances speech finally come out last night? He couldn't be sure. The spoken word was fine as far as it went, as clean but as evanescent as this new technology stuff. You simply couldn't hold it in your hand.

In a few moments the off-licence would be open and he would try again to make the note-taking principle transfer.

Boychester, Boychester. There was a rum customer. A bad one these days and getting worse all the time, what with Sizer and the Rotary and all. Since his elevation he thought he owned you just because some of your writing went in "his" newspaper – "I carried an article on this . . . I initiated a piece on that . . ." Initiated. What sort of a word was that? As for himself, he couldn't write his way out of a paper bag, for all his plausible talk.

These were not like the old days, wild great old days when you could get a simple respect with your writing and no-one tangled you up in all this rubbish about televisions. Print was print and made of metal; ink was ink; and you didn't have these odd Sizer fish lurking behind every rock.

"Me and James Crowley and a fine motor to the coast knocked spots off the Vindicator," he said in Mr. Parnell's direction. "Crowley and me on the cliff edge soon as the story broke, him with his camera case blowing back like a scarf in the gale, me with my pad and pencil, and both of us leaning out like bowsprits on the wind nearly to Inisheer just for a glimpse of the wreck."

He reached down for his socks and boots and put them on. "And when the wind dropped dead I was inland a yard but Crowley went down head first 400 feet. They got his camera and his body. Greatest pictures on God's earth. And James Crowley, a fine cut of a man, and 35, is mulching down in Ballivaghan while Boychester struts. It is not at all right now, is it, Mr. Parnell?"

The wheel squeaked that it wasn't and Cathal gathered up his jacket. He looked for a moment as if he were cradling it like a lost son, before saying: "We need a stiffener, you and me both. Let's go." He slung it round his shoulders, saluted Mr. Parnell and opened the door to leave. A bus was sneezing into gear round the corner where the route turned to head back into central London. A West Indian conductor was arguing with an Irish boy. On the landing Cathal could hear the first wisps of a badly played flute. A familiar cadence came and he watched as the gas pipes trembled with the E, more and more at every repetition.

"That's my boy, David," he said as he went down the stairs. "You're a Jewish bastard and you're evil and parent-rich but you don't give a toss for that and you live in an E flat and you don't care for Boychester."

He walked on to the foot of the stairs in his perfect exile, far away from the victimising past, and out into the glare of County Kilburn. Halfway down the front steps where he had crawled naked an hour earlier he felt a coarse itching around his groin and an unnatural tightness on his hips. He looked down and said: "Jesus! Pants on over trousers!", then scurried back up again as the nuns returned into view round the corner

* * *

Upstairs in his identical cell Camina had dreamed deeply and vividly again in the night. Sitting on the bed directly above where Cathal had ranted at the dwarf, he was trying to shake himself free from the nightmare. It had been the same one again. It was in the First War and he had been Isaac Rosenberg in the trenches, the only real war poet not in the officer class. The sergeant barking at him had had an orange face and a tiny round badge on the lapel of his khaki. The sergeant was shouting that Rosenberg had not marched as far as the other privates, of which he was the most junior; but every time he tried to step up his pace he slipped from the duckboards into the quagmire of mud and corpses. He held his rifle above his head, as his training had taught him. As the mud bubbled at his nostrils and he prepared his last and longest breath his body convulsed and he woke into Camina.

This must have happened three times or more; back into sleep and the same warscape, and the same sergeant clearing into vision out of the dark. Each time he had been half frightened to bob back under into sleep, because of the phantom waiting to draw him down by the ankles. But each time he had let himself succumb in curiosity and the hope of something more.

Camina's room was tidier than the one below, which was not hard. A suit was on the hanger behind the door. In a new chest of drawers that smelled of landlord's standard issue he had his own pictures. There were a dozen of them in a roll, violent abstracts of bombed cities and more recently one of the recurring sergeant at the Somme.

He lay full-length on the bed again and stretched his eyes wide open to let in as much daylight as would enter. Gradually the sergeant receded.

On the wall behind the bed, where many another

passionate and private young man might have had a crucifix, Camina had two photographs of Rosenberg taken just before the outbreak of war when the doomed poet was in his early twenties. In one of them he was staring out wanly from a summer outing with a group of his fellow pupils from the Slade. There were picnic hampers and wine bottles and bicycles on the grass, and the limbs of the girls in their long dresses had settled in a way that made Camina wonder whether promiscuity was really as new as his parents had always claimed. Rosenberg looked as though they were causing him nothing but pain. There were bluff lads in the back row with moustaches and strong chests under their shirts. Rosenberg looked older in the face than he was, but his body was frail and vulnerable.

In the other photo he was a few years younger still and standing on a wharf with three of the other Whitechapel boys, Simy Weinstein, Joseph Leftwich and John Rodker. Under the bravado that has patinated every picture everywhere of four young men was again the deep Yiddish gloom, the forlornness that had come over with their immigrant fathers from Russia. Rodker had a large gold ring in one ear, and it kept its gleam in the print.

Somewhere among Rosenberg's features in both pictures was the tentative look of a young man who nearly belonged, and who wanted above all things to do so. Camina too yearned to be lifted on a spirit of corporate rebellion and self-knowledge. He deeply resented the fact that it was his father and not he who had strived all through the Depression for his status at the bar and who could look back from his autumn in Hampstead Garden Suburb with a poignant pleasure at the lean years. How many times had the young David Camina listened through the floor as his father and his successful friends, Pavlovsky,

Roether and the rest, had recalled their struggles; the first break, the early days of the theatrical agency, Jacob's little hotel, Sacha's landing of the Government contract for the radio parts.

Nobody realised, in the days of consolidation and thanksgiving, that every expensive toy at Christmas, every latest board game from Sacha was a slight to his independence. Board games for an only child; the rich unkindness of it. Every January, just before term began, when David slouched sadly about the big house, his mother would take out Sacha's game, assemble its complex pieces on the floor and read aloud from the small print of the manual. Then, rather formally, they would throw the dice and move the pieces mournfully about on the colourful expanse. Kneeling there with his mother, with the clock ticking away the last of his holidays, and the two of them trying to wrest some chequered ocean from each other – this was the stuff of perfect sadness.

Then there were the endless hours of study with the Rabbi before Bar Mitzvah, a ceremony at which he had felt more alone than ever; a little man, an official adult yet hardly pubescent, reeling off by rote the wisdom of another time. There could have been no more certain way of sealing the alienation between them and him than that moment of his receipt into their world. After the ceremony there was the rib-digging and cheek-tweeking from Sacha and the others. Little David was a man now and was being bound and laid with kindly violence into the mould of the professions. Doctor, accountant, lawyer – it mattered little. With the crushing support of more than enough money, David would be successful or somebody's heart would break.

Upstairs in his bedroom, with the sounds of a dinner

party coming up from below, he would open his book of Rosenberg at the full-page plate and set it on his easel before the mirror. Then he would turn off the centre light and place himself about three paces behind the stand so that from where he was the face in the photo and his own looked almost the same size in the glass. He would incline his head a fraction to the right to match the print, and then compare them. They were roughly the same shape, with long bony noses and slightly protruding ears. There was no hair visible on Rosenberg because of his private's cap, so Camina had palmed his own curls back from the temples in both hands. It was not at the eyes but at the mouth that the resemblance seemed to dim. Where Camina's had an almost pouting weakness about it, Rosenberg's had been hardened and brutalised by army life.

When he left home he was 20 and a source of great chagrin to his parents. He had taken none of the baits of his father's connections. He had done a series of menial jobs – in a glue factory, a bookshop, a restaurant, and then finally, after a last attempt at parental guidance, nine months of an austere business course in Lyons.

When he had returned, and mooched around the house for a fortnight, he announced that he was joining the *Bugle*, and Boychester. The new editor had been full of largesse, until the opening of a file, the running of a finger down a printed scale, and the offer of a miserable wage. Still, it was a job.

"I would have hoped, David," his mother had said.

"Th-that what, mother?"

"Well, that you could have spared me a little more of your time."

"How much, mother?"

"Well, two years. Not more. I wouldn't ask for more. Your father is away so much."

"He should cut down."

"I know, David, but you know what he's like."

"Do I?"

When he had moved into the flat that smelled of gas, the mother inwardly saw it as a flight abroad, though she said to her friends that he was living in West Hampstead. It was as much Kilburn as anything could be. Instead of phoning him at work, she would write him long letters with news of the neighbours' children, and sometimes a pair of socks. The four miles that separated them had acquired the distance of oceans that keep whole cultures apart. If ever she drove south into London to shop, she would take a wide detour to preserve her ignorance. At home everything in his room was kept as when he had been there. Camina showed Cathal the letters and they christened their squalid rooming house The Trenches.

Today Camina was feeling more buoyant than of late. Perhaps it was the weather, but more likely it was the knowledge that the weekend was here, which meant two days without Boychester.

He got dressed as he heard Cathal scraping about below like a rodent, and shouting at Mr. Parnell. The two men left their rooms at the same time and met on the landing as Cathal was pulling the key from the lock with some difficulty.

"Is everything all right?" asked Camina.

"Morning, David. Yes thank you. Parnell put a curse on my clothes. Are you for the High Road?"

"Yes."

They walked down the bottom flight of stairs to the front door. In the hallway was a dining table with a broken flap. On the top was a litter of old circulars, some glossy ones stapled into polythene, and unopened envelopes. Many of them had the names of people long gone to no forwarding address. There was a Mr. A. Quirk, whose letters from Barclays Bank were almost daily now, and a Bharat Patel, whose supply of British Medical Gazettes stood at six.

"Ghosts are slipping a bit, no?" said Cathal. "It's a bad thing when a man neglects his mail. Should we mark them 'Lost in the Trenches' and send them on to the War Office?"

"The War Office?"

From the bottom of the front steps a stench like old fruit hit them as they stepped into the daylight. It came from the mound of plastic bags that had been piling up for the three weeks of the dustmen's strike.

"More of your older dead is my guess," said Cathal. "That tin I recognise from a month ago. Smelled foul then and a spell of burial's not doing a great deal for it. Dead Man's Dump was your man's poem?"

They picked their way down the path and through a rotting gate that dragged on the concrete. "You're down in the mouth, Camina. Boychester bringing you down? Look, he gets me down and all, but he's not worth the air for fussing over."

"I'm all right."

"Funny dreams again? That ghost of yours. Were you around with him in the night?"

Camina said nothing and they walked on in silence. Eventually Cathal said: "You know, David, when all those nobs like Rupert Brooke were whining away like lads of the manor with their bollocks caught on the paddock railing, our lot were laughing themselves hoarse in Dublin."

He pinched the bridge of his nose in mock-suffering: "'Oh fie, oh woe. My plot, my shire . . .' and fellows like your poor funny little Bantam were getting their arses shot off to keep those cunts with the whip hand. Oldest fucking story. But listen, David, we all have our day, Yids the same as dogs, and there's no two-bit television men can hog the thunder for good."

The words were spoken with passion, almost as if they were a prophecy based on a tip-off, and Camina brightened a little. They rounded the corner into the High Road, leaving the Trenches in the care of the dead poet and the statesman who clung to life by a hamster. They were soon caught up in the crowd of Saturday morning shoppers. There were young mothers yelling at babies as the prams spilled shopping on to the pavements, and stunned-looking pensioners with a carrier bag and a crumpled list.

The two picked their way through the throng, the younger one locked in his familiar paralysis, and the other with his fiery bowel that was one day to drop its magnificent contents, when the constipation cleared.

"Cheer up, now," said Cathal. "Look. There's a fellow laughing at Boychester in the *Bugle* if only he knew it. Oh, Camina. We are racehorses, you and me. Well, so we are presently slung between the shafts of a milk float. So what'll we do? We'll make the damned thing rattle a bit."

They walked on, the upward lad who wouldn't come up, and the downward devil who wouldn't go down.

III
Conversions

ON A MORNING three weeks later, another in the blazing spell that showed up every sweaty pock in this part of town, two very different surprises were making their way through the dust to The Towers and The Trenches.

Boychester was down early to answer the doorbell. Facing him on the step was a spotty youth in a tee-shirt with a rude slogan on the front. He had a crate in his arms and a piece of paper in his teeth.

"Mr. Boychester?"

"I am he."

"Vine's Wines."

"Indeed?"

"For you, sir."

"For me?"

"Could you sign for it?"

"Sign?"

"Guv'nor insists. Thinks we might nick the stuff otherwise."

"And might you?"

"If you could just sign at the bottom here, sir."

He stuck his head forward to be relieved of the paper, but Boychester didn't move. Instead he motioned to the step with his eyes, for the crate to be placed there. The youth did so grudgingly, then plucked the paper extravagantly from his teeth and handed it across.

"Thank you," said the master of The Towers. With the youth's biro he scribbled his signature, a huge florid B tailing off almost immediately to a flat ripple, and returned the sheet. After the youth had snatched it and left, Boychester looked down at the crate, which contained twelve wine bottles with red tops. He dragged it across the mat, panting with the effort. Tucked down between the shoulders of two bottles was a note. It read: "To the best Bugler in the borough. Bless you. Bobsy."

Bobsy Marshall was the fat chairwoman of a residents' association that had started up in Brondesbury. Her husband was away in West Africa for a chemicals company most of the time, and this childless frump looked in vain for affairs. Now her energy was going into committees and fund-raisings of every description. Lifeboats, orphans and endangered species – these were among the items selected to shore up her sense of social indispensability. She was belonging earnestly to the voluntary sector whose contribution cannot be measured. As far as the association was concerned, her stock-in-trade was litter petitions, tree-planting campaigns and street parties. On the new headed paper she had written to Boychester for publicity. Two weeks later a story appeared called "Bobsy Bids to Keep Brent Blooming." It had been "initiated" to Pam, but for some reason it was to Boychester that the thank-you present now came.

He looked out influentially across the street as he calculated the rough value of the gift. On the opposite pavement a group of self-assured little girls were filing into Larch Towers. Their school hats were mostly hanging round their necks by the elastic. Two or three carried tiny violin cases.

He was joined in the doorway by Mrs. Boychester and, a yard behind her, George.

"Any mail, darling?" said his wife.

"Mail, no," he replied.

"Nothing for me or Jogger?"

"And to whom did George write that he expects correspondence?" The boy put his thumb in his mouth and skulked back towards the stairs. "Something for nothing is an abject fancy, my lad, and an idle one in this world."

His wife spied the crate on the carpet and squealed: "Wine. Boychy, all that wine! Where from?"

"A small token of gratitude from one who has much to be grateful for. Bobsy Marshall. Of the association."

"Clever Boychy!"

It was the folded journals and bank statements to the departed which made most of the noise on the hall floor of The Trenches. But it was a thin brown envelope, full of purpose, which made Cathal's eyes start as he rummaged among the paper foliage at his ankles. For it was addressed to him. What could this be? A letter from Dublin perhaps? A relative getting in touch after years of silence and wanting somewhere to stay while in London, and over-estimating Cathal's circumstances entirely.

That was the danger of giving an inflated account of yourself to a distant family. Some of them thought it was actually more than propaganda. Possibly that awful nephew, Liam was it, who asked all those awkward questions. Well, he would have to take his chance with the rest in the guest houses of Paddington and Shepherd's Bush.

He wriggled his thumb into the corner of the envelope. This was a strange, rather exciting intrusion into such a complete exile. No bank account meant no letters from the bank. No householder's status meant no rate demands. No phone meant no phone bills. And a gas meter meant no correspondence from the Gas Board. Unadorned survival like this could be carried on quite insulated from the clamour of creditors. The Greek landlord got a roll of notes in his hand every week and that was that. So who was this making a penetration via the letter-box?

There was an official looking crest on the top of the page. Casting his eye quickly down to the bottom he glimpsed two kinds of typing, one bolder than the other. "Sufferinjeezuz, the police," he yelled. "Christ-on-the-Cross! What the . . ."

He dropped the piece of paper to the ground, as if ignorance of it could make it null and void, like the rest of the pressing demands on the floor.

Cathal was a quick reader, and his eye, if not his brain, had taken in the contents at a stroke. Now what? He was in a state of mild shock, without a doubt. He could simply write "Not Known Here" on the envelope and re-post it, banishing it, at least for the time being, to the ether of bureaucracy. Or he could reply with a polite note, dissociating himself from it completely. Then again, he could let it fester with the ghosts. One way or another, surely he could prevent himself from being dragged down the humiliating path that was being pointed to by the letter. An ulcerous old loudmouth he may be. He would admit to that in open court, and more.

The drink; he would gladly own up to that as well, yes and the abuse meted out in the Chairmen, such of it as he could remember.

But baring his arse to a pair of passing nuns – the indecent exposure of which he now stood accused, for Heaven's sake – that was another thing entirely. What if one of the Irish papers picked it up and ran it in Dublin? All the relatives there and in the area of the country editions would see it for sure. "So, Cathal, who has made London his oyster and who is the pearl in the middle of it, is done for flashing his butt at holy women. Well, now we know, don't we. Up in court in a place called Willesden."

Cathal composed himself a little and thought of the dignified approach. He could come clean and write letters of apology. He would pin them to every tree in the borough, if that was what they wanted: "C. Dwyer, The Trenches, hereby regrets offending Sisters Whatever-Their-Names-Are through the unwitting exposure of his fundament. He retracts it."

After all, that was what it was all about, wasn't it? The two nuns passing that morning when he was stretching naked down the steps for the papers – they'd been and shopped him. And them from an Irish order, almost certainly, if they lived in the convent a couple of roads down. That was the worst of it. Of course, and then they had been coming back the other way when he'd been leaving the house a little while later, with his pants outside his trousers.

He was still too numbed to check his worst fears against a re-reading of the letter. Besides, the more surmises he made, of the grimmest kind, the more the emerging reality appeared to be worthy of them. This was getting to be like Camina's nightmare, an amphibious sort of creature that could inhabit the day as well as the night. Far from sliding out of the fingers when grasped, it stuck like putty.

But that morning, whenever it was – days ago? weeks? he couldn't be certain. Surely he hadn't said anything abusive to the nuns. Or was that the first long-dreaded occasion when something meant only as a thought had broken into sound?

The whole incident seemed remote to the point of ghostliness, a half-remembered dream which would seem very familiar again when it recurred, but which in the meantime didn't belong in the light at all.

Cathal could just remember that on the morning in question he and Camina had gone down the High Road together. It had been one of the first of the very hot days, because he could still see the glare of the white arms from summer dresses on their first outings of the year. But that had been after the nuns. Working back, he could remember, but oh so dimly, the itching between his legs and the funny tightness around his hips. Before that, what? He had been shouting at Mr. Parnell and had thrown his jacket all over the cage. But the previous night had been a gruelling one in the Chairmen.

He struggled hard now in the hall to muscle all these fragments into some kind of chronology. Not that his command of them was likely to make an ounce of difference now. They had their own order, with dates and times and a precision that was not to be compromised by other people's imperfect assemblages of the facts. They would advance, as sure as Sizer.

For certain on the morning in question Cathal would have been hung over to the point of intoxication, with not enough time between the last draught and the waking up to clear his veins of the stuff. On most bad mornings he could feel it re-activating heavily at the first exertions of his heartbeat. So what must it have been like then? Technically he had probably been drunk.

The shock gave way to panic. Now that his tiny indiscretion was being picked and teased at by officials – pen-pushing coppers in shirt sleeves, chuckling to each other as they put his sheet to one side of the desk – there was perhaps nothing at all he could do. The process now started would gather momentum. It was a cancer as malignant as progress, and as indifferent to the feelings of the body through which it was passing. It would come on.

The panic was getting a purchase on him. He raked through the rest of the mail on the floor, looking for the reprieve. One of the other brown envelopes would contain the letter countermanding the one in his pocket, and this present reality would be sent back into the night. But no; three long buff ones, each with white panels stuck onto the front carrying the address; bloody circulars, yet more magazines folded in half by a waistband of brown paper; great thick publications full of colour and advertising, expensively printed at a Swedish plant; another dire warning to Mr. Quirk from the bank manager talking now of bailiffs and the other blue murders of the bureaucrat at the end of his tether; a postcard with four square views of Marbella, from what looked like Brian and Lydia, to an unheard-of ghost.

But none with the reprieve. A mistake possibly. Reprieve only posted after original. Clerical error down at the station. He would ring from work and sort this out, informally if necessary. Mrs. Weekes would know the station officer. No, better leave Mrs. Weekes out of this.

Cathal toyed with the comic touch. What about a letter back with "Your ref: You, My Ref: Me". Possibly. No, a policeman would be calling to speak to him. Better not burn his boats before then. He let out a grunt of frustration. So the church and the law had got him by the throat, one on each side, just as they'd got Charles Parnell a century before, and were marching him towards the hurdle for a public dragging across the cobbles. He thought, with the usual relief, of Maire and the Chairmen, and the rationality that would come with the first one of the day.

Camina might have an idea. The lad could be heard coming down the stairs. He appeared round the landing and slumped his way down the bottom flight. He was pale and unslept, and was fiddling with the buttons of his shirt.

"Bad night, David?" said Cathal.

Camina didn't answer.

"Sergeant been playing up on the bridge?"

"I – I couldn't sleep."

"So it looks."

"I couldn't sleep at all."

"Never mind, lad. Weekend soon. And listen, tomorrow night there's a band up at Biddy Mulligans with my old dead friend Crowley's brother on the fiddle. Cheer up, David."

They walked down the front steps, the flight suddenly at the centre of things, and set off towards the *Bugle* in silence. Eventually Cathal said: "The milk cart is rattling a bit, David."

"How's that?"

"Not quite how I meant it."

"Oh?"

"I'll tell you in the Chairmen."

In Holborn on Monday morning a brace of skeletons rattled down the corridors of the head office. They were as old as the human technology can get. A scrap dealer would have offered you a fiver for the lot and lucky to get it. A harder man would have charged you for taking them off your hands. They would have told you these models were so old that no-one was making the spares for them any more and that the next time something went wrong, that would be it.

But then people had been saying that about the skeletons for goodness knows how long; yet each year, come the AGM or some other important function they rattled in from Maidenhead or Aylesbury or Sunningdale to take their seats. And today was definitely an important day. None more so.

Skeleton Hubbard was the oldest but most spritely of them all. The paper group was started in 1830 and it was widely thought that Hubbard, then a young man in his thirties, had founded it. People were reluctant to abandon the theory, even though it would mean that he had now passed his 180th year. In fact the founder had been his great-grandfather. This man's picture on the board room wall bore such a likeness to the present Hubbard (in a way there was no likeness, just identicality) that you would have sworn the living one had just had his portrait done. The two intervening Hubbards were also on the wall. Captured at the same age, they were surely not mere relatives but two more images of the same man. When people in the firm spoke of "the old man" they meant whichever one you wanted them to mean, and the four identities had been elided into one as if by a trick of time. When the old man did this or that in 1880, it was the present skeleton Hubbard, and when the old man said this or that the other day it was just as likely the forbear on the wall. Striplings of 60 had spent years plotting for their own small preferment in the firm on the death of whichever old man was there at the time. But these deaths dragged imminence across spans of maybe two decades, by which time the upstarts were long turned to dust. In Cathal's words, the old man was "a restatement of age."

He was heading the rest of the skeletons towards the board room with as good a gait as he would have had if he had ever been young. Slightly behind him was a man of similar age, but in worse repair. He seemed to be walking with an extremely complicated limp. It made his right arm thrust out behind him and his left leg take a colossal stride which brought the head down to waist height. Then the right arm would shoot through and he would slowly drag himself vertical and start again. Occasionally, when the body was parallel with the ground he would fix his eyes far down the corridor and shout: "Curl boy, curl. That's the style!" When he bent forward every bone in his back pointed through the jacket as in a species of armadillo.

Hubbard glanced over his shoulder and said to him: "Going well, Tom. Bang on target. Wockingham Bowling Club'll be proud of you on Saturday. Round of applause for Tombola there, gentlemen, please."

Old Tom had been declared dead years ago by the younger men in the firm. In fact his funeral had taken a prominent place in company mythology. If you had not been at Tom's funeral, you were no-one. If you had not seen the people and the drunken indiscretions on that occasion, you were sadly adrift. Stories begat stories and what had not happened there was not worth happening. There was the directors-in-the-duckpond story, the one about Jack Rimney's morning coat, and a host of others. Tom's funeral was a home of time and occasion for all unplaced tales. The difficulty was that it had never taken place outside the minds of the "guests" and every time Hubbard appeared in Holborn, there was Tom like a ghost at his shoulder. Some said there really was a haunting going on. Some decided this was in fact not Tom, or else just ignored his presence. A simple accounts clerk told him how much everyone had enjoyed the last funeral, and when was the next one to be? As doors opened now and faces peeped out at the procession, an old secretary whispered: "But he's been dead for years."

Today was special on two counts. The Royal Progress of Skeletons on this 150th anniversary was reason enough to feel a sense of occasion. It was a rare privilege for the drones of the *Bugle* group to see their ultimate lords in the flesh, if you could call it that. More than that, it was the day when all the mysteries of the new technology were to be revealed. Sizer was ready in the board room at the big table with the men from Compucomp. The cut-glass tumblers were upside down in place on the decanters of water and the firm had been released for the morning to attend the briefing. Already more than 150 people were packed round the panelled walls and on the rows of folding wooden seats. The mongers of the new were to meet and disarm the slaves of the old.

But there was one more important confrontation today, which was acting itself out in the attic of Hubbard's skull. Today two of his oldest and most immutable principles were locked in civil war: they were the opposition to change – and the profit motive. In a straight fight only a fool would have put money on the first principle. Yet what was afoot in the industry, and in this very building therefore, was so revolutionary, so utterly different from anything before, that there were grounds for opposing it out of shock alone. Hubbard's mind was, for the first time in its endless life, open.

The minds of the other four were as closed as ever; closed as only dry old sponges can be when left without the irrigation of blood for years. Hubbard would decide what was best. There was still a world of wisdom in those nimble old cells, particularly when it came to determining the profitable course. He was a Platonic rather than a Patrician Tory; he believed with a religious conviction in the drone class and his ineligibility to it. As for other religious beliefs, there was more than a hint of Boychesterism. No-one could have lived for 180 years without realising that church, change and profit were a close-knit Trinity. Perhaps he would not have underwritten Cathal's description of the clergy as "the wet-nurse of usury," but there were people in this building who would swear that whatever tune was played in church, the old man would be singing this verse, even if it didn't fit:

> The rich man in his castle
> The poor man at his gate
> God made the high and lowly
> And ordered their estate.

So his open mind was only open for being twice closed; once to the thought that a death knell was tolling for a system centuries old, and once to the horror of having to pay more than the going rate for overheads.

The skeleton train rattled round a right-angle in the corridor and then right again in single file into the board room, Hubbard leading. He had never seen the room so full. Normally there was just the table in the centre of the green carpet, with not another soul until you came to the old man on the wall. Even important retirement parties had not brought numbers this large. Hubbard was a little thrown to see them all here – the secretaries, the printers, the journalists, the accounts people; all the elements usually dealt with separately. He took them in at a glance.

There were those, like the secretaries, on whom patronage had worked well for generations. Nothing, not even the most meagre wages, could shake them from their loyalty to "the company." They were dedicated to this thing beyond the call of masochism. For 150 years they had been feeding the mouth that bit them. You could have told them they were subsidising the profits of the skeletons and they would have smiled proudly back. A hamper at Christmas was more than enough to nip any sense of exploitation in the bud. Hubbard took them in.

In another knot were the journalists. A study in disarray, thought the old man. Full of busyness in other people's rights and other bodies' inefficiencies, while their own union dues fell into hopeless arrears. Aim at them rather than the printers and you were picking the easier fight.

There, right at the back, was that fiery Irishman who always smelled of drink, and that self-important one with the orange face. And the woman with all the court cases. And the young Jewish one. Hubbard took them in.

Further round were a few of the printers down from Kilburn, a very few of them. The low number was no doubt a statement that the new technology was a matter for them to decide, not the management. There was the oldish one who had led the last pay negotiations, a cantankerous machine minder who always made a point of turning up in his overalls, even if he had not come from work. "Our fingers on the button, Mr 'Ubbard" had been his slogan during the talks in this very room. Hubbard took him in.

There was something unsettling about seeing them all gathered here now as though they were uniting against a common enemy, and ready to swap notes on tactics.

This was all Sizer's idea. He had better make sure it was a good one. The skeletons moved towards their seats behind the table, Tom still bobbing and bowling.

Standing beside the table was Sizer, clasping one hand nervously in the other. He had an immaculate suit on, electric blue, with lapels falling sleek and sheer. An unusually large clipboard was under his arm. "Power plank," thought Cathal at the back.

Sizer gave an obsequious smile as Hubbard approached, and moved forward to help the old man into his seat at the centre of the row. Hubbard waved him away and said: "Good house, Sizer. Don't waste it now."

Near Sizer was a smaller table at which sat the two men from Compucomp and a woman of about 24 who looked out of place. She too had a clipboard and was dressed rather like a waitress, with a very short skirt. Her name was typed on a little badge pinned to her blouse.

Hubbard settled down in the leather chair and looked at his triplet predecessors on the wall. No need to ask them what they were thinking. Their thoughts would be the same as his. They were his. He lived in their minds and they in his.

Sizer cleared his throat and stepped forward a pace. In

his best Rotary voice he began: "Gentlemen. No, ladies and gentlemen. We live in momentary times."

"Momentous, you dolt," said Hubbard under his breath.

"In momentous times . . . in which we are living from moment to moment. The minute hand turns on the clock and unless we watch it very closely the hour passes."

He paused and looked down at his notes.

"In the beginning was Caxton, William Caxton. Possibly Bill to his friends."

He glanced up for a laugh that didn't come. "Or even before him was . . . this." He picked up his exhibit A from the table.

"That's right, gentlemen, a duck's feather with . . ."

"Pheasant's," muttered Hubbard.

"A pheasant's feather with a pointed tip. The scribe or clerk would place the tip in . . . this . . . correct again, a bottle of ink, and scribble whatever it was he was so inclined to scribble and who are we to say what that might or might not have been – on a piece of parchment which alas I have been unable to procure.

"Now then, I want you if you can to picture the dismay on his face when Mr. Caxton – our friend Bill – came on the scene. Here was this clerk or scribe scribbling away when the door bursts open and in comes this chappie saying: 'Aha there. You're using the old technology. It so happens that I've invented a press, and you my friend are redundant, not in the sense of being without a job at this moment in time, but of going to be in that situation ere long, come and work for me.'

"Well, gentlemen, we can't pretend that our little scribbling man banged down his feather there and then and said 'You're on,' because he didn't. No, no, these things don't happen overnight. But you can bet your tunic, or whatever, that friend scribe very soon said to himself: 'Stuff this for a laugh, I'm going over to Caxton.'

"And you know, he was right, because if he hadn't gone over to Caxton, Caxton would have gone over him, so to speak."

The man in overalls shifted feet and folded his arms.

"Because one thing which we cannot ignore in this life is progress. I say openly and sincerely to you that if you – any of you – can really, honestly look at progress and say, effectively, words which amount to: 'I can get on fine without you, sunshine,' then you are a better man, or woman, than I am, Genghis Khan."

"Gunga Din." Hubbard groaned audibly.

Sizer cleared his throat again and persevered.

"As you can imagine, pretty soon our clerk chappie was, as you might say, with the Woolwich, that is, Mr. Caxton. The jolly old quill still had its place I expect, for signing expenses and things like that (no laughter), but when it came to books, then the press was the thing. That was progress for you, and I am submitting to you that the changes were for the by and large better.

"Today, gentlemen, we are in the middle of a similar revolution and must grab the challenges it furnishes in a double-handed fashion."

The coming man's rhetoric was going badly wrong.

"For if we do not, then it will pass us by and someone else will cash in. And we don't want that to happen, do we. Of course we don't.

"Apart from anything else, you can't keep a machine going – any machine, don't care what it is – take your car if you like – beyond a certain age. You know as well as I do that come the anno domini our faithful motor, Merc or Mini, will go the way of . . . of this. That's right, our old friend the quill. Gentlemen, today we are in that anno domini with regard to our printing capabilities."

Here Sizer paused for effect and thumbed through the pages on the clipboard. The man in overalls was looking impatient. Behind the big table Hubbard was as impassive as his three reflections. At the other end of the room Cathal's vision was still shaking from the weekend. Sizer looked to him more than ever like a maladjusted TV set. "Someone turn him off, Camina, no?" he whispered to his left. "He is making my teeth scream and he should be turned to darkness."

Old Tom's head was still bobbing extravagantly, not with bowling now, but with sleep. It was rising up backwards in an arc around his shoulder and stretching the neck with its weight until every old tube and duct was showing through like a specimen for autopsy. Then the head swung down again, a bulb whirled from a flex, and somehow just pulled up in time to avoid shattering on the felt top.

"So, gentlemen," Sizer ploughed on, "now that our printing works is going the way of the old car and the quill, we must swim with the new or sink with the old."

Cathal muttered to Camina again: "Sizer is not up to this. It is a pig's ear he is making."

The coming man fumbled again for the grand manner but splashed into a bog of mixed metaphors and misquotes. By now there was a low buzz hanging over the room and a swapping of puzzled looks by the staff in their groups. Still he slogged on: "You see, the sword of Damascus is over us and we . . . we are beneath it. It is glinting in the sun with the promise of plenty and a better life for all of us."

His voice rose half an octave and his speech quickened: "We cannot ignore it. Better we bow our heads to bathe joyously in the blood of progress because you see they just don't make the parts any more. My department is up against impossible odds. Manufacturers laugh in my face when I tell them the state of our machinery. Only the other day, Tuesday I think it was, there was a fellow up from the London College of Printing and he said to me, Mr. Sizer he said, you should have got this sorted out years ago – you're in dead trouble, mate – if you don't modernise someone around here will set up their own plant and that'll be goodnight to you and your funny old Heath Robinson things with their greasy wheels and rubber bands; oh yes I've heard all the sentimental drivel about dying crafts and all that eyewash, but sentimental doesn't ring the tills does it, and it's your head on the block . . . well he was a reasonable man and in the trade for 30 years, and what answer do your union worthies have to stuff that doesn't work any more – personally I'm a paid-up member of the NGA and I don't like to see fellows slung out of work any more than you do but what's so clever about making things so bad that there's no work left for anyone just because for years they've been having it so cushy and picking up £200 a week for standing about, and that's before you take into account all those dodgy pay packets marked Mickey Mouse and L. Piggott, Tattenham Corner; look, in a few years' time even the new gear will be kaput and we'll have to think again. In Japan I think it is, they're already working on a system that can take in what you say on a microphone and turn it into print just like that and then it puts it all onto a page automatically, no mucking about with all that ink and metal . . . just think of it, and of course knowing the Nips that stuff is going to be at the trade fairs any day now before you can say Yamaha, with its beautiful micro-circuitry all tidy in a box and little white keys on the side."

The man in overalls was leaving the room with what was meant to be dignity. This meant a broad, raw-boned walk, with legs almost making an A-shape, and fists clenched. He paused for a second in front of the table and turned to face the room. With a throw of his chin he motioned his handful of mates to join him. While they seeped from the crowd he turned to look on the row of skeletons. Their eyes blinked and flickered behind thick lenses. Old Tom's coconut had fallen from the stall. His head was flat on the table, and from it the thin wire of the neck traced back into the hollow of the collar and the suit in search of some anchorage in the bone-work. The impression the row gave was of a vandalised old computer on half current.

The man in overalls looked at it from one end to the other, then fixed on the one steady gaze in the middle. The eyes were blue and even young, and the skin under the chin, although old, didn't wrinkle and bag like the others.

"Mr. 'Ubbard sir," said the union man. "I respect you as a gentleman and wish to inform you on behalf of the Imperial Chapel that you are doing the company no service by giving us . . . this." He pointed to Sizer, who was about to start again.

"We have had our differences in the past, sir, and shall again, I do not doubt it, in the future, but they are differences which can only be inflamed by this kind of talk."

The buzz over the room died a little as this new conversation at the front became apparent. The union man sensed it and said a little louder: "If this man has his problems, I am sorry for him. But he is not helping himself.

Mr. 'Ubbard sir, mark my words. God – and Mammon for that matter – and Mammon, helps those as helps themselves. You know it in your way and I know it in mine."

He tapped his finger with an unexpected lightness on the edge of the table, before marching to the door with his men in tow. They were aping his walk and wearing strong chins to underline his statement.

"Round one to the noble savage," said Cathal to Camina at the back.

Sizer did not seem to know or care about the exodus. A wild glint started in his eye and his gaze seemed to be locked at some point above the ceiling.

"Brothers," he began again, "we are on the ground floor of nothing less than a miracle. Let the moaners moan and the carpers carp, but let us also not be among their number. For who will not follow when He bids us come?"

The two Compucomp men and their girl swapped embarrassed looks which might have said: "We know we're good, but this is a bit over the top." They shifted in their seats.

"The benign hand bids us enter the Promised Land, where brother against brother – which is what we've been having in the past, let's face it – is no more, where all is clean and bright, and where the Satanic rivers of ink and their boulders of metal cannot enter, where columns of light deflect the dark stream's course into the desert of the dead feather, the rusting car and the linotype machine."

Sizer was now panting, and his right arm was beaming a message from wall to wall. He shouted: "Heed ye the prophet and the profit shall be yours!"

Hubbard was on his feet. There was an intake of breath from where the secretaries sat. Some of the journalists were laughing and shaking their heads.

Now Hubbard and the Compucomp men were converging on Sizer from either side. The larger of the two was about to grab him round the waist from behind, when Hubbard said: "Stay there if you wouldn't mind. I understand you are to speak next."

"Yes sir, but . . ."

"But nothing. You stay at your post. You want the contract, I take it?"

Very gently the old man pinched Sizer's elbow in his hand and walked him towards the door through which the printers had just left. "Come on, old chap," he whispered. "You've done your bit."

Suddenly Sizer was sobbing like a baby, with one hand pressed hard against his forehead, and his face drooping. His feet slouched as he was led away.

"I must tell them, sir," he said. "I had to tell them the only truth."

"Course you did, my boy."

"Someone had to."

"And you did. Indeed you did."

Boychester looked on in dismay as his contact with the action left. Some of the orange drained from his cheeks and the mouth sagged into a glum triangle.

At the door Hubbard turned and said: "My apologies. If you would be kind enough to wait two minutes, I should be grateful."

He herded his charge out. The Compucomp man who was to speak next looked to his partner for some guidance, but the partner was blank. Cheryl, the clipboard girl, was smiling sickly like a hostess on a plummeting DC 10.

It was hardly more than 30 seconds before Hubbard returned, having sat Sizer down in the rest room. He walked with a straight bearing to the middle of the table, but this time he stood in front of it.

He had taken charge.

"I would ask you for your patience for a short time," he began.

It was a deep, dignified voice, resonant not from the chest but from the throat, and seemed to come from a point near every listener. But there was a sadness in it that showed in the falling tone at the end of the sentences. It touched the tail of all that he said. Nothing that he spoke could escape the cadence.

"I seek your co-operation on only two points this morning, ladies and gentlemen. Firstly, that you do not judge too harshly the speaker you have just heard. His has been the most difficult of positions. We should not mock him when pressure and passion combine to undo his equilibrium for a moment. The occasion may have unsettled his judgement, but the remarks were not entirely without substance."

"The old devil should be in advertising," whispered Cathal. "He is putting tin foil round a turd and we're buying it as a truffle. It is brilliant."

"Could any of us here swear that we have never at any time given a weighted picture of an argument because of our too zealous commitment to one of the strands? Mmm? I doubt it.

"The second point on which I ask your co-operation is this: that you keep an open mind on the prospect of change until you have absorbed all the evidence available. One thing we may have learned this morning is that conservatism and its forces do not enjoy a monopoly on prejudice."

It was a sound performance by the old man. Three

minutes earlier chaos had threatened to take over. Now he had managed to salvage something like order from the wreckage of Sizer.

"These are mad and erratic times," he went on. "Yes, one might be forgiven for believing that to behave in an aberrant fashion is to act in concert with the spirit that prevails."

"Don't miss this, Camina," said Cathal. "Now he is blowing his besmirched rep's nose for him. The fellow is no amateur. Don't you love his lies? I love to hear them."

"Perhaps enough of Caxton for one day, ladies and gentlemen. Better we content ourselves with the knowledge that we are indeed in a secondary phase of the industrial revolution. The first speaker was correct here. In a moment you will hear from the gentleman on my right the precise implications of this. Let me end by urging you to resist the extremisms of Luddite and technocrat alike. The truth, as always, occupies the middle ground. My thanks to you."

A few pairs of hands clapped as Hubbard went back to his seat. Then the applause spread from the middle of the room and broadened to the edges until it became nearly an ovation. Mrs. Weekes was smacking her hands together lustily as if she was applauding some act of retribution by an old judge at the quarter sessions. She looked around her and even groovy Harvey and Pam were clapping. Only the Irishman and the Jew were motionless. Cathal's thoughts were on Maire and the clock. Another piece of sales talk to sit through, and all under the guise of enlightenment. A sop to participation, the whole business. Give some tuppenny ha'penny filing clerk the idea that if he doesn't like the colour of a cable then the whole system won't be bought.

The applause died down. Even old Tom had woken and was hazarding a clap. His hands passed each other in the air with some force and jerked his arms back around his trunk like a straitjacket.

From then on it was downhill all the way. If Hubbard and the end of Sizer had been the peak of the sentence, now came the falling-away, the small print under the bold clause.

The Compucomp man made a brave start. He had the blinds drawn and snapped his fingers at Cheryl, who flashed a slide from the projector onto the screen. As he hurtled off into his patter he clicked his fingers again and another slide of a woman at a keyboard came up. It was blurred and upside down. Cheryl tried to re-focus the machine and the square of light darted all over the wall from floor to ceiling. It caught old Tom full in the face. It lit his eyes with horror and threw the shadow of his skull and waving hands on to the wall behind in a terrible shaking image. Then it passed on and left him in the dark.

The Compucomp man, Stuart Sturridge was his name, made some crack about old technology and waited for the "*lumière* to catch up with the *son*." Cheryl would get an earful later.

Before dozing off in the semi-darkness with his back against the wall, Cathal thought hard about Maire. He stretched his wrist forward out of the cuff and glanced at the watch. Maire would have drawn the bolts. The Chairmen would have that sweet sordid smell of hops and tobacco, almost a clean smell when taken with the breath of disinfectant that hung in the air. Certainly a smell that meant a beginning rather than an end. The old boy from the library would be in there with his *Telegraph* crossword. He would be saying to Maire: "Stars take direction from the dairy – five and three, first letter of the second word, W." A wet rag would have been passed over the rexine and the early shift of men from the building site would have arrived, thirsty as dust.

Almost as he slipped into sleep Cathal noticed how uncannily like Sizer this new speaker was: the same glasses dominating the face, the same square but boneless lines underneath. Another screen, whatever his blessed name was, another TV set. The likeness had not escaped the others in the room. The drone of his voice in the half-light, the monotonous plastic click of the projector, the stupefying list of figures and data that issued from him – all these things had the effect of making it seem as though Sizer had never left the room, that his outburst had been an illusion, and that here he was now merely going through his paces properly.

"The sport is all past," thought Cathal. "Sizer is laundered and restored. He has risen again. He is back at the heart of things, cutting slices for us if we are lucky and don't fart in the lift. He is a bore."

Cathal's head lolled back against the wall. Somewhere he heard: "The VDTs or video display terminals key in the data to the central bank, from where it can be called up."

Sizer was not going to explode again. The new model was properly earthed and insulated. How dull and worthy was this tract of information. Every assertion was documented. There were figures, long specifications with letters and obliques, and more slides. Perhaps the next one would be interesting. How long did one have to wait for one of a bishop in the bath or even a stag at bay against some russet glen. Anything but this. Cheryl, click. Another diagram. More pipes leading out of a box marked "workplace", with arrows going to smaller boxes at the edge of the screen. "With a front-end system and single-key stroking, the

VDT operator, once he has coded himself in, can scroll up at will. Character absorption rates of course vary with the system, as does delayed response."

Cheryl, click. The small print had taken over. This was no type face for a human interest story. Sizer's explosion, for all its absurdity, was worth ten of this. That had impact, or whatever the word was that Boychester's Buyers would use. But what did this have? Nothing beyond undiluted facts and the promise of more. Just like life: a constant assertion of drab realities, punctuated every so often by an orgasm of bile and mischief. It ground you down in the end, to see all your flares fall and fizzle in the river. A progress of mud. Flaherty had remarked the same, had he not, in his celebrated monologue, even though that had been prompted by a more specific sense of grievance. But the metaphor held. Cathal tapped the heavy lining of his jacket. Flaherty was eloquent but would need tidying up a bit. Part of him must be taken from the drawer this afternoon and matched up with the parts in the lining. The splicing was long overdue. The man had been rambling and would be brought to book. And he would be presented first to the toilet wall in the Chairmen and then to Mr. Parnell himself. Cheryl, click. "This is an enlargement of the micro-circuitry found in . . ." Cathal's plug was drawn from the socket.

His was not the only chin that lolled on its chest, nor the only nose that snored and snorted in great gusts. The birth of the New Sizer's Enlightened Age was being celebrated in a temple of boredom.

For the polite and the curious the whole occasion started to inflict the physical pain that waits at the far boundary of tedium like this. The symptoms were presenting in different ways. One ad rep felt an ant right in the middle of his brain. He stuck a finger deep into his ear until it ached, but the ant danced on in the core. A tele-ad girl could not control her right leg. It vibrated out of control, whether she put it across the other knee or rested there on the floor. The accounts clerk next to her had a terrible ache in the pit of the stomach. He tried to ease it by shifting in his seat, but it hung on grimly. There was only one cure for all the sufferers, and it was a simple one – an end to the talk.

When this moment came at last, with its release to every cramped limb in the room, Hubbard started a round of polite applause. He roused his old colleagues and they joined the stunned and blinking crowd that was pushing towards the door.

A secretary was saying to her friend: "I still don't understand it at all, love," and the friend replied: "Don't worry, dear. No-one does."

A middle-aged journalist said to another one: "So when do we find all this stuff on our desks, then?"

"Not a clue," was the answer. "Depends on the printers."

After this hard morning all the groups made for lunch; Hubbard and the new Sizer to talk systems, Boychester to meet his Buyer for an afternoon of importance, Mrs. Weekes to an emergent Pinkie, and Cathal to knock his wayward orator into shape.

That evening in the Chairmen the Irishman was himself again – almost. The police letter still burnt a hole in his pocket and in his head, but the Clearances speech was forming nicely. Tonight was ripe for its release. Camina was with him, withdrawn and morose as ever.

Back at the *Bugle* in the afternoon it had become obvious to Cathal that the best part of Flaherty was gone from the drawer. Now he mulled over the fate of his creation. When he told Camina that Boychester had got him and was holding him captive, he meant it as a purely emotional truth. But when Camina didn't question it, it seemed plausible, and in the two hours that he had sat in the pub the metaphor had hardened into fact.

He went to the bar for the next round, and to tell Mick.

"Mick," he said. "Boychester has some of Flaherty."

"Oh," said the landlord, clearly puzzled, but realising that it was something of importance. "That's a bad business then."

"It is, Mick. It is."

Maire's fat little chin wobbled on her hands as she shook her head in confusion.

While Cathal and Camina had been deep in talk the pub had become crowded. On the way back to his seat Cathal noticed two familiar figures sitting next to each other against the opposite wall. They were Ron Wheeler and Joan something from the council. They were both PRs, and apparently at the start of a surreptitious affair. What else would have brought them here? Joan looked like the Queen and sounded the same, particularly in the Chairmen, where her voice came like a clarion through the coarser tones. Ron Wheeler was a horse-faced beanpole of a man, still wearing his thick suede coat, despite the weather, to plump himself about the chest and shoulders. They nudged each other and whispered as Cathal passed, and although he pretended not to notice them he thought he detected a look of mockery in their faces. It was a Mrs. Weekes look, the kind worn by self-righteous onlookers so often at the back of the magistrate's court.

He remarked on it to Camina, and as the evening went by Cathal had the ever-strengthening thought that if the two weren't actually in league with Boychester over Flaherty, then at the very least they knew all about the police letter and the nuns. Whenever a gap appeared in the thicket of drinkers at the centre of the room, he could see them there, closer to each other every time, giggling in his direction.

The juke box seemed to be growing louder by the minute, with its odd mixture of Irish songs and old pop tunes. Cathal was raising his voice to be heard. "You see, Camina," he was saying. "This is the nature of the game. When one Sizer goes fut, they just roll up another one, identical. And there's more and more where that came from."

The knot of drinkers shifted again and the PRs came into view. It seemed to Cathal that Joan had actually been pointing and gesturing and had lowered her hand on realising she was spotted. He was also certain she had mouthed the word "nuns" twice, and Ron Wheeler had tutted.

Camina was suddenly aware of Cathal slamming his glass on the table and making off across the room. He was wading through the thicket like a man fighting for the door of a tube. The PRs looked up in horror as he reached them. He was leaning over their table in a predatory way, the eagle rather than the terrier. Camina was now at his elbow and could just hear him say: "And how is the Umpteenth Estate? Slumming it, I see?"

Joan kept her composure and said: "Am I right in thinking you do not hold our profession in very high regard?"

Cathal shouted above the noise: "Is it not enough to be

a pampered turncoat and play Cerberus to a bunch of crooks, but you want respect as well?"

"I didn't quite say that, Mr. Dwyer."

"You didn't have to, dear. Oh, but you must have been an earnest little filly once, all puffed up with council bashing. And what now? Taken the mayor's shilling. Yes sir, no sir, I'll keep it from them. I'll set a false scent. *Ils ne passeront pas!*"

"You do have a most fanciful picture of the whole business, you know," said Joan.

"Fanciful be fucked, Missus. I know your tricks. All the pretending to be on our side – our little Mrs. Mole – all the skittering off to warn the chiefs to be unavailable, all the closing ranks and the transferring of the callers until they get lost in the dark of the GPO. I know the lot, the whole lot."

"Oh this is a quite blissful job description," said Joan. "But not one that I recognise, I fear."

"Then look in the mirror!" Cathal shouted. "Oh Jesus, but there never was such a conspiracy against the laity as your lot. And all because they pay you over the odds and make a fuss of you at Christmas. What a trade this is. To say a thing is precisely, but precisely what it is not, for the fooling of them that have every right to know. To call a spade a silver fucking trowel. You're a pox and a bedsore and you know it."

Joan looked as professional as she could, which was quite a lot. She was clearly about to give Cathal as good as she was getting, when Ron Wheeler chimed in with a piece of poor man's galanterie.

"I – I think," he said nervously, "that Joan does a very good job under very trying circumstances."

"And what a testimony is that," said Cathal. "A very

good job under very trying circumstances!" He was yelling almost into the man's ear. "And where were you before you started plugging the Gas Board's leaks for them that you are such a certain referee? Well?"

Ron Wheeler looked down at his shoes and shifted on his seat, as he had clearly done often before when this question had come up.

"Don't let him put you down, Ron," said Joan. "Go on. Tell him."

Wheeler muttered something up at Cathal with what was meant to be defiance; but it was inaudible.

"Louder!" Cathal demanded.

"I said, 'The Complete House Plant'."

Even over the noise of the juke box a high squeal of air and liquid under great pressure could be heard. Then a shaft of beer shot from Cathal's mouth and nose. Most of it hit the mirror behind the PRs and started running down like helpless tears. But the rest fell in a fine film that made them duck and blink.

Quickly Joan was standing up, brushing down her pleated skirt and beckoning to Ron Wheeler to join her. This he did, rubbing away from his eyes what seemed to be more than beer. They disappeared through the throng towards the door.

Cathal made off in the other direction, towards the back alley. The melancholy was settling again already. It seemed to come sooner and sooner every time.

In the foul-smelling lavatory at the back of the building he swayed with his legs apart and one arm held straight out against the wall above the urinal. Outside the door was the usual splatter of fresh sick, a display of diced vegetables that had got nowhere near digestion.

The little cell was painted black, through which flakes

of plaster showed. A greasy string knotted at the end hung from the cistern up in the corner. From the tub came a constant dripping of water which was wearing away the wall in a straight column. Through the drips Cathal could hear the bass throb from the juke box. It was a version of "Thousands Are Sailing to America," smoothed over and upholstered by the arranger. The voices were self-consciously tangy with Irish, but not a word of the lyrics could be heard.

It came through the wall and down the alley in a monotonous 6/8 time. All the modal eeriness and the grace notes of the original, which Cathal had known from babyhood, were knocked off for the rock market. The fiddle should have been soaring and darting, but it was rooted on one shrill pitch for bar upon bar. Something about the insistence at the bottom of the register made him nearly want to sing, but his heart would have none of it. Somewhere along the way these lads from the south had been headed off by their man in the record company with his smart suit and his knowledge of the market. They had got London and a pocketful of tin in return for a smudged air. Progress of mud. A flute had entered the mess somewhere, with a bogus fall. Now there was a drone beneath the bass, from a synthesiser. What should have been a climax of sadness and glory was being pushed by force of wattage to an empty crescendo. The throb stopped with a showy abruptness and the fiddle hung on for seconds. Then another coin went in and the tune started again.

Cathal shook his head and clenched his whole face. These self-professing Irishmen in London would accept such an insult. That was the worst of it. This was now the kind of music which they would board as a bark to carry them home in an ecstasy of false nostalgia. The English had infiltrated so far that this threadbare stuff was good enough for them to wave as a standard. The notes that Crowley's brothers had flung outwards and upwards in a reel until the whole sky and coast danced to its raggedness were now trussed up like a battery bird. A kicking mule was reined up and groomed for the indoors, and the poteen was nine parts water.

With his mind's ear Cathal tried to retrieve the clean bone of the tune, but the arrangement had altered its whole being. More coming men with gadgetry had called in the old cards and dealt out a pack of new ones. Look where you would, no-one was making the old parts.

He banged the wall with his fist and let out a moan. The melancholy was gathering again. A pair of worthless PRs abused. Self-aggrandising pygmies possibly, but surely not worth such an input of emotion. So many cues for aggression staring him in the face and he could manage nothing better than to bring down clay pigeons with his mouth. Somewhere a few miles away Hubbard and the new Sizer would be talking money, buying and selling the new system in whose boundaries everyone would have to live. Perhaps a nib was signing "Hubbard" on a document, the new Sizer poised with his blotter. That was the quiet epicentre of the storm, yet here was Cathal blowing about in the tails of the cloak that it flapped. He should have been represented at the signing, telling the signatories that there was a human price to good business, instead of castigating civic lackeys. It was sickening, to be so silent as the cake was being cut into uneven quarters, but so noisy at the irrelevant fringes of the table.

Still, Flaherty was in two, and that was grave. Part of him was still heavy in the lining of the jacket, but another part was being compromised by the moment through his imprisonment in Boychester. There was no doubt that Boychester had got him, none whatsoever. Flaherty, who could not be got back by heart, was even now in the sow suit, and yielding up half his oratory to a fat waist.

Worse still, the proper place for that dialogue was occupied by the wretched police letter. It insinuated its way into clutches of pound notes and Partition script, and leered up at Cathal like a grim little changeling.

Cathal shook the last drop from his member and strode furiously back down the alley and into the bar.

Before he knew what he was doing he had climbed on to a table in a lull after the juke box and was standing on the top like a knock-kneed Colossus. His hands were on his hips and he was shouting: "Gentlemen! We are now in the time of the Fourth Clearance!"

The bar went silent and someone asked: "Is it last orders already?" Two men just in from the street were looking at Mick as if he was a police officer about to intervene. He shushed them with a finger and Cathal went on: "The Fourth Clearance – and by Christ the worst! Now then, the first you know of. It was the Cheviot, with my Lord Sutherland tugging him borderwards by the fleece. Some said he would not endure the first winter. But he did: and he tupped away mightily with his dirty shit-hung old arse hammering the air, until there was a thousand more of him to gainsay the prophecy.

"It was an occupation of white, seeping up the map like maggots. Here was new technology if you like. A minimum of fuss were Mr. and Mrs. Cheviot. Just got on with the business of chewing the grass, proliferating and getting slaughtered. A life cycle beautiful in its symmetry and rich in self-denial: feeding, breeding and bleeding."

Flaherty in full flow at the Abbey could not have wished

for a better audience. Even the two sides of beef in the corner sat looking up at him with expressions that were near to meekness.

"Not an ebb in view. Rank after rank of bobbing backs. Food for the army, wool for the gentry, and penury for the people in the way. Course, his lordship called it an "improvement," and who am I to contradict him? However, them that didn't quite see it like that had their houses burned down for their trouble. Off to the coast. There to fish. Beyond them, nothing but the sea, which they looked down at past their toes and wondered just how you do go about harnessing the salmon for the plough.

"The evidence of your ears is correct, gentlemen. Thousands did go sailing to America, but not aboard the lush vessel in that juke box but on a reeking old orange crate, mostly holes, and nothing but rats to plug them with. Yes, thousands did go sailing when his lordship's coffers swelled them off the map with the blessing of the clergy."

"Don't know what the man's talking about myself, but it has a good ring to it," said one side of beef.

"He's in the papers and he has a way with his words," said the other. They emptied their pints and waited for the Second Clearance.

"The Second Clearance," Cathal began again, "came with the stag. Where royalty stalks its pleasure, let no man dare to turn an honest ploughshare, lest he get a bullet in the head.

"Is there a new technology here, you are asking yourselves. Well, in a manner of speaking yes there is, if you will only keep in mind the importance of the greatest return for the smallest fuss. And here the new Sizer and Hubbard himself – possibly not persons known to you all – could learn a thing or two. For you see all that is required of him is that he goes down with a manly bellow when shot and that subsequently he surrenders his head as a trophy without resistance. Oh, sheep were good but this fellow is even better. Put a few of him on the estate and charge the Yanks and Danes any sum you will for a week of shooting. Thousands are flying from America for the privilege."

It might have been the passion in his voice, the frenzy of his movements, or a bit of each which kept his audience. Perhaps it was just the sight of a man on a table in a pub delivering his thesis on the Clearances at high speed. Whatever it was, Orator Dwyer had now been on his platform for five minutes, and below him necks were locked for more. Mick, with his elbows on the bar, was serving no more drinks.

"Third Clearance will not detain you long," said Cathal. "This one sounds almost like the reverse – but I tell you it is a Clearance nonetheless of peace and sanity in pursuit of a quick return. What else am I talking about but the oil? Crime up, sickness up, filth up" – the cathedralling arm was touching the lamp – "and modest stillness down, down and down. Life in a slick is a grand life for them that live in the offices of the city."

For that moment the Chairmen could have been the site of a Chartist rally and Cathal Feargus O'Connor himself at the height of his powers. There were shouts of "Hear Hear" from around the walls, and even the ones who had not a clue what he was talking about (which was most of them) were buoyed along by the sheer commitment of it all.

"The sheep, the deer, the oil. The sharp end of the new status quo gores the belly of the tried order, and for the benefit of none but them at the safe end of the spear. His Lordship is graven in stone for his eternal glory, the Duke of Westminster grows fatter still from Yankee huntsmen's dues, and the oil chiefs know of no bank strong enough to hold their money. Like I say, we are here in the time of the Fourth Clearance – and it belongs to Mr. New Sizer and his flock of dry white letters."

It was an imaginative leap that could only cause more confusion, but the listeners kept faith.

"Unchecked and unstemmed, they are coming up the screen, scrolling up in line after line. They are worse than the sheep are Sizer's maggots. You cannot pull them by the coat, nor crook them at the neck. You may set a dog at them and he will whine in fear. You may shoot at them and they will rise on as if they never saw you. You can claw at the screen until your nails tear, but Sizer's maggots will not break rank or slacken their pace. You can even stop their heart at the current until the image fades, but they will hide in the dark and wait for day. I tell you there is no way of dealing with them. They come like ghosts and they don't break a twig or stroke a blade of glass. They take up no space, they make no noise, no smell, no taste. When they pass out of view there is another battalion of the same called up from the bowels of a warehouse with no walls and no location . . ."

His voice rose to the climax: "We are un-kneed, un-thighed, neutered, gnawed and numbed as they climb, and only New Sizer grows fat as King Worm on the grains of bone. In a word, gentlemen, I do not like them, I do not want them, I do not need them. I am against them!"

Cathal had resumed his Colossus pose and from his mouth hurled an Icarus of beer spittle which seemed to gather size as it rolled through the air and splatted on the lino behind the bar.

"Fifth Clearance coming up, Cathal!" Mick yelled, and rang the bell. "Your very last orders gentlemen if you please."

As suddenly as he had gained their attention, Cathal now lost it. At his waist the heads and shoulders and outstretched arms were packing forwards to the bar. One edge of the table lifted under the pressure. He stepped down shakily and was lost in the tide. The Colossus was just another boulder being bullied along by the stream. Back in the progress of mud.

"I touched the lamp, Camina," he said.

"You did, Cathal, I saw you."

"No. I mean really touched it. The flare on top of the dung heap. I lit it."

"Yes, Cathal."

The two were packed tight into the press of drinkers, every one of whom was trying to push a glass into Maire's face.

"And then I blew it utterly," said Cathal.

"H-how?"

"Well, the whole damn'd thing was about Scotland."

"So?"

"I can't stick the Scots."

"It was better than either of the Sizers."

"The Sizers and me, David. We have this in common. No-one takes a blind bit of notice. Except that Sizer and his maggots win in the end while I'm arsing around down the dead men. I feel sick. I'm cutting out."

The two of them squeezed their way back against the tide. Eventually they were outside on the pavement, moving away from the group that seeped out from the doorway and stood for a while around the gutter, bemused, not talking. One side of beef was relieving himself into the gutter and humming the tune from the juke box. From inside the pub the same air in a different key, which was bass and cracked beyond identification, was barging a way out.

Cathal and Camina braced themselves for the high note that loomed. It came with a sickening belly roar as from a shed full of cows in the night in the last agonies of poisoning.

"Lads are in harmony again," said Cathal as they moved out of earshot. "They'll never get the same note, not on anything. All roar and danger and knock-me-down."

The sound was baffled almost into silence as they turned the corner and left the island shaking with self-destruction. By the time they got to The Trenches Cathal had been hit with hammer blows by the fresh air and was lurching morosely against the gate, which gave way. It hung like a broken wing from the bottom hinge. He barged it out of the way and it scraped open to a right-angle. Something moving caught his eye by the bottom step. It looked like a spreading carpet of white dust, moving across the path from the rubbish. He blinked hard and steadied himself on the gate post like someone trying to clear an itch from the cornea.

"Maggots," he growled.

"Where?" said Camina, craning forward.

"All over the shop."

"Forget Sizer and the screens, Cathal. Please. We've had a night of it."

"No, real ones, lad. Beautiful little wriggling Rotary rice, marching from the rubbish."

"Where are they going?"

"Everywhere in general and nowhere in particular. I think it's just a show of strength. A tattoo, sort of."

"How did they get there?"

"Same way as Sizer's. Out of nowhere. A germ. There's millions of them."

Wherever he looked on the path, against the wall, up the steps, all over the split bellies of the plastic bags and the mess inside them, the little grains were teeming.

"We've caught them in their dressage, I think, Lieutenant Camina. Boiling water if you please."

"Yes, captain," said Camina. He ran up the front steps and opened the door. A few minutes later he reappeared with a large saucepan which was slurping boiling water from the brim. Below, Cathal was dancing in a wild jig from one foot to the other, arms reeling up and down around his ears. At each stamp he was shouting: "Boychester, Sizer, Boychester, Sizer!"

Camina sent the water spilling across the path under Cathal's feet. A thousand maggots died in the first wave. Some died instantly, but there were other hardier ones who were jacknifing like little fat men doing exercises.

In the kitchen on the landing below the rooms all four rings of the cooker were at full flame, covered by more saucepans and a huge red casserole. Camina ran up and down with each one as they came to the boil, then filled them again from the thin tube of water that came from the geyser.

Outside in the front line Cathal danced on with a splash. "Come Dancing comes to you tonight from The Trenches Ballroom, Kilburn," he was shouting. "Cathal Dwyer, who is a hairdresser by day and loves the Bee Gees, has sewn on all his own sequins and ripped them off again as they made him look like a poofter. His tweed is hand-woven and scented with Johnnie Walker. Cathal is dancing his own arrangement of the Maggotty Two Step."

Camina had produced a broom and was wooshing the corpses down the path past the Irishman. They flowed through the broken gate, across the pavement and into the gutter. Soon a river flecked with white was flooding down to the drain.

"Thousands are sailing," said Cathal. "That's the style. Keep them coming. Dead in transit." He was growling the melody from the pub, whooping and kicking between the lines. "There goes the big fellow that got the beans."

After half an hour of sweeping and stamping, the cracked tiles of the path were shinier than they had ever been. A few little corpses lay twitching under the stars on the black bags, and the rest seemed to have fled downwards in terror. Cathal slumped down with his haunches on the backs of his heels and wiped his brow with a sleeve. His trousers were dark with water up to the knees. With a finger he scooped out the last of the maggots from his turn-ups. Camina leant on the broom handle and panted.

Cathal seemed close to exhaustion. "Now there's the way to deal with Sizer's lot," he panted. "Boil them and broom them and send them on their way."

In silence they looked at the shining pathway. "Can be done," he said at last. "Can be done."

Two lovers strolled past the gate where the nuns had walked on the Saturday morning. They too looked in, not at a bare arse stretching down for the papers, but at the curious sight of two clearance workers blowing with an exertion that had a strange violence for the time of night. They checked their pace and looked at the figures lit by the glow from the bare bulb in the hallway, and at the saucepans on the steps. She wore a smart skirt and a pair of high heels which she was lifting high on the wet pavement. He was hurrying her on with an arm round her waist.

"Been to a dance?" said Cathal to them over the gate. "I been to a dance and all. Grand dance. Dance of Death. Charge of the White Brigade."

"Come on, darling," said the young man to the girl.

"Night, dear," said Cathal after them. "Good breeding."

There was a breathy "well, really" from the girl, and their steps clicked off down the pavement. The two soldiers stood in silence again. After a while they gathered up the pans and trod slowly up into the house. In this hot weather the place smelled more than ever of gas. The ghosts' letters on the hall table looked utterly dead and lost for messages as if the gas had got to them during the hours of exposure. The veinwork of pipes still moaned and grumbled from its part in the slaughter.

They climbed the stairs. The air was hotter still from the cooker in the kitchen, still firing on all rings. Camina turned them off. Carrying on up, he saw that Cathal had slumped down against the wall in a sort of crouch.

"I'm for bed, Cathal," he said, and dragged himself past. "Good night."

Cathal didn't answer. He stayed there motionless, the head drooping, and listened to Camina's footsteps on the stairs. They halted at the top. Then there was the metal rummaging of the key in the lock and another silence followed by the door closing and Camina walking in. Here the steps were hollow, like someone tapping the inside of a cardboard box. A couple of minutes later there was the faintest squeak of a bed spring and then nothing more.

In the quiet, which seemed huge and lonely after the maggots and the pub, Cathal slowly rose to his feet. He staggered through the door of his room and began to undress: one shoe yanked up to the other knee, the fingers fumbling for the knot, then abandoning it and scraping the thing off by the heel with the toe of the other foot. When he tried to remove his jacket it caught him in a kind of half nelson. With one arm trussed back like a chicken wing he spun round and round in a circle, chasing his elbow with his teeth. He became a blur of check to Mr. Parnell, in a spin that was just as violent as the hamster's own. Suddenly he lost his footing and tumbled to the floor against the side of the bed, like a plane crashed onto its nose and wing. There he lay snoring heavily until morning.

No sooner had Camina lolled into sleep upstairs than he was on the bridge again with the sergeant; the sea of mud all round them as far as the eye could see was lumpy with bodies. This time the sergeant was standing beside a very complicated piece of weaponry. It was gleaming with bright new paint, and beside it on the duckboards were the pieces of the packing case in which it had arrived. Behind the sergeant were two smart men in civilian dress, with spectacles and clipboards. They two had the small shiny wheels on their lapels. One of them had a sheet with an intricate diagram in one hand and was pointing backwards and forwards from it to the screen on the rear of the machine. Next to Rosenberg was another ragged and exhausted corporal, an older man, and the two of them were being addressed in sharp barks by the sergeant: "You two there. I want you to take all this in. We have taken delivery of a dozen and you will be operating this one. Clear?"

The older man was muttering "I'll not handle it" under his breath and the sergeant was working himself up into an orgasm of rage, jumping up and down until the boards rattled, and pointing at half a soldier whose jaw and torso were sticking up from the mud. Now one of the civilians was pulling levers and twisting little knurled wheels on the device. The top part of it was swivelling like a massive trunk towards the corporals and the air was becoming intense with heat and a painful glare that was overpowering them with nausea.

At this point all through the night Camina would wake in a freezing sweat and try to shake away the picture by thinking of meadows and milk and flowers. But the dream only came stalking after him, poaching into his tiny corner of wakefulness and clawing him back down onto the boards and the carnage, for more of that terrible radiation.

IV
Inspections

THE FOLLOWING FRIDAY at about 3.30 Boychester in the sow suit, bound for Weybridge, was baking to a turn on the platform of an almost empty Brondesbury Station. He was well fed and watered and trying to put a favourable gloss on the impact he had just made on the new Sizer over lunch.

The train from Broad Street was already so late that the next to appear wouldn't be that one at all, but the one coming after. This little line that clung to life, a staple clipped over the north of London, had been the subject of many Boychester leaders. He quoted inwardly: "This surely is not one of those services that should be asked to stand or fall by its own viability."

He was not so sure now. His tune was changing with every minute that passed. With a hoot and a smelly roar a diesel dragging 20 tankers to Willesden crawled by the platform at walking pace. A hundred yards away a signal fell and the train squealed to a halt, front and back sticking out at either end of the station. A shudder ran along the snake of metal tubes like a multiple pile-up. It was as if this filthy tramp of a thing was deliberately baring its backside at the editor from its place ahead of him in the queue. The heat shimmered from the tanker tops in waves. Down the platform a West Indian guard was on the phone in his little box. His voice was rising to a frenzy and he was jigging about behind the glass.

Boychester looked at his watch. The line was not worthy of preservation and would be condemned in the next leader, the other metal beast permitting.

As the goods train wheezed and creaked and thought about moving, Boychester walked into the little waiting room. It smelled of urine and one wall was sprayed with graffiti that read: "Rip off, skive, and be cruel to creeps." It was cooler in here among the squalor. To Boychester it was preferable to the reek of the train.

He mulled over the lunch with Sturridge. It had followed a more or less identical course to the first one. The similarities of the two men were so great that Boychester could remember betraying surprise when Sturridge mentioned in passing that he had been taken on by Hubbard to do Sizer's job. It had never occurred to Boychester that he wasn't in that position already.

The scenario – that word had come up again and again – had not been unlike the Mark One version: namely, that progress with one hand would put screens where there were once typewriters, and with the other would tumble the island site like a pile of cans. What could or would happen to Boychester was touched on by Sturridge only in the most tangential way. And here he was more menacing than the old Sizer had ever been. That man had certainly fancied his projections and was in love with the notion of classified data. But Sturridge knew even better that there came a time when power accrued in proportion to information hoarded.

The guard shouted something and the train jolted forward. The tankers passed the window of the waiting room, sluggishly picking up speed, and Boychester heard the refrain of a nursery rhyme run involuntarily through his head with the rhythm of the wheels. It was something that his wife had always sung to George in her breathy contralto. It took Boychester a while to identify the snatch. He had little place for music. By this time the train had disappeared and was audible only as a low rumble, with the occasional noise like a knife being sheared across the rails. "Down will come cradle, baby and all" was the tune in his head. Or was it the other way round: "Baby, cradle and all." The words replaced by a new set which edged their way in as if taking a dancer from her partner. They went: "Down will come Boychester, *Bugle* and all," and the perfect fit of them made him wince.

He walked briskly out of the waiting room and on to the rising heat of the platform. The goods train had now clattered into a rhythm on the down gradient out of sight, and the noise was coming back in fragments from the walls of the houses, the ground and the sky. But still the barbed little refrain wouldn't clear from Boychester's head. It made him rake with a fine comb over what Sturridge had said to bring on this panic. But there was nothing. There had been – and this was really the only possible cue for alarm – that remark about the timing of the change-over. How had it gone? "Once the head goes, the body will follow." Something like that. Then there had been the same image taken up again over coffee: "Every cat knows that once the shoulders are through the gap, the rest goes easily." The earlier Sizer had never had such an interest in the cryptic mode. Playing around with the crockery had been his way towards an analogy. Boychester shuddered as he remembered those pudgy fingers swinging the sugar bowl across the debris to the ash-tray of Holborn.

Boychester loitered thoughtfully along the platform, head bowed to contemplate the true meaning of it all. The head first and the body following. At the time he had taken it as a specific allusion to timing, meaning that once the new technology was in, the rest, including the fate of Boychester's paper and its premises, would follow. But there had been something else in Sturridge's manner which, in spite of his harder and more professional patina, had allowed the editor to stop short before rounding off the dreadful equation. Quite what it was he couldn't be sure, but it tempered his gloom with hope. If he felt he had achieved anything at the lunch, it was to persuade Sturridge that he was a man of breeding and civility. Weren't these the qualities to cut glass with coming men, the traits to which they also aspired?

So there had been much "sirring" during the meal, and much talk of Weybridge, the father-in-law, his circle of friends; all those badges which he hoped would clip together and form a membership card to the Cut Above. In fact Sturridge had been struck by Boychester's apparent disowning of himself and the real furniture of his life in favour of the Weybridge connection. Why, he had asked himself, was he being treated to so many details about the life and style of the family into which this strange fellow had married.

However baffling his tactics to impress Sturridge had been, Boychester had matured since the first Sizer lunch. No elementary gaffes this time, no ill-planted smears to deflect blame. He had found himself across the table from the one chosen to usher in the new way, and it was not a chance to be squandered. There was still more than a hint of resentment that he should have to pay his dues to a mere technocrat, but the pragmatist was rising in Boychester.

He must court the proper lieutenant, otherwise . . . "Down will come Boychester, *Bugle* and all." The refrain entered him again.

At last the little yellow face of the train, with its code B4, came into view on the right, and the three-coach unit squealed to a halt. There was a time when this poor cousin of a line had run every 15 minutes, with six coaches. Cut, literally cut in half by Beeching's blade and reduced to three an hour, it now sidled apologetically between Broad Street and Richmond as though scared of detection. It went unacknowledged on tube and SR maps alike. Even the stations had a ghostly existence. The smaller ones had no guards, only blackboards with "Pay other end" in chalk. These had been denounced by Boychester as a "Dodgers' Charter."

He climbed into a single compartment in the middle carriage. The seats in this old rolling stock were scarred and stitched like a face in a seat-belt advertisement. Next to a scrawl of praise for Arsenal were the words "Virgin's last hope" with an arrow pointing to the communication cord.

Boychester settled in by the window. After a few more stations the train pulled out of Willesden Junction and nosed slowly round a big leftward arc. Through the window he could see the expanse of Wormwood Scrubs, with its football pitches mapped out between the tiny staples of the goals. Beyond them were the regimented low buildings of the prison, and further away still the tower blocks where Boychester's readers were racked up into the sky. Highest of all was an ugly one of perhaps 30 storeys. The lift shaft was set apart from it and joined by tiny concrete passages, as if it was trying to do its work at a distance. This was the "sky prison" of another Boychester leader after vandals had short-circuited the lift cables by smashing the hydrant on the top floor. He quoted inwardly again: "350 feet of GLC masonry encases the hostages of today's delinquency."

A hundred yards from the track the jib of a crane was shaking with the weight of an old car which it was swinging through the air on a magnetic claw. The car landed among the other scrap in the breaker's yard and the jib swung back round for its next load. The refrain started up in Boychester's head once more, to the rhythm of the train.

The huge vista disappeared behind a building for a second and then re-emerged. Right at the back was the candle of the Post Office Tower and then the greyer lines of the Westminster Bank block at Liverpool Street. Even to Boychester the view spoke of new shapes thrusting up arrogantly out of the decay. For just a moment he was moved by the indifference of it all, the utter disregard of the new order for the old. Those square and functional forms; what did they have in common with the streets they peered down on, except for a jealous eyeing of the space? Sturridge's image came back to him. "Once the head is through, the body will follow." Those shapes were coming up and up out of the ground like worms, and it was just a matter of time before they would be crowned with gloating heads. If you stood at the bottom and sneered you would be lost in the shadow and forgotten.

In his mind's eye Boychester could see Sturridge's great cat standing like a Hollywood artefact in the memorial garden, pawing through the window of his office and splintering the brickwork on either side, just to get its huge shoulders through.

As the saner proportions of Acton asserted themselves

and darkened the compartment, he relaxed a little. Weybridge was less than an hour away. The mother-in-law would meet him at the station and they would speed back to Tamarisk Lodge through the half-country of Surrey. There Boychester would be expansive and genial with whatever guests were at the house. There was always someone. He would be the charming but modest son-in-law, down to top up his batteries after another week of discharging high office with restraint.

The train was clattering and galloping. It was here, between Willesden and Acton, that it could still get up a head of speed, almost like a real train. For the briefest second the houses split for the last time on to the panorama. By now the alignment of the landmarks had all changed for being seen from further south. The engine managed a broken hoot and dived down again between the back gardens.

To Boychester, who was being shaken like a dessert on a trolley, these sharp apertures on to the view were like the shutter of a camera. The sudden light dinned the image of that sprawl into his brain, where it stayed until the next perspective shot through. Even now, with the green train folded deep in Acton, the picture remained of that great swathe of city, and of Boychester's little constituency lodged somewhere in the moulding.

The train threaded through Gunnersbury and Kew in its scurry down the side of the metropolis. Boychester could feel a physical sense of relief to be getting further and further from Sturridge and all the other riddles of that domain. Time stood still at Tamarisk Lodge.

There was a different noise of the train on the girder bridge across the river. When it landed on the other side it was looking down from its high banking on to leafy gardens and a tennis court of clean orange. Through the other window was a building like a massive wedding cake with four tiers, but tapering in from the broadest one at the top to the narrowest at the bottom, all on a solid concrete plinth. Behind the tiny windows of the Public Records Office were rows of books and papers shielded from the light. Boychester had read about it somewhere. Government documents were stored inside and grew like moss along the shelves at a rate of 100 yards a year. Military records, law reports, DOE projections, statistical surveys were all put out to grass here for the scrutiny of anyone with an eternity to spare. He formulated a comment for it: "A standing invitation to democracy's inspectorate." Yet the thought of that unstoppable advance of evidence frightened him a little. He was sweating again. Nothing shielded from the porer. He thought of Mrs. Weekes, and of her own little stockpile of crimes. He thought too of Cathal's strange character, still so inscrutable in his pocket.

The yellow face of the train nosed sharply round to the right and under a road bridge. It was running parallel to the SR line out of Waterloo. They were being overhauled by a smart blue and white train bound for Reading. It moved swiftly past Boychester's window with the sound of wind in a corridor. One of its pick-up shoes kicked sparks from the rail; then the back of the last coach whistled by and swept on through Richmond Station as the people on the platform drew back. Not for the first time in recent months Boychester had the sensation of trying to join a motorway in a pony trap. His own train clanked ever more slowly towards the buffers. It felt as if there was a switch-point at every yard. His carriage was being thrown from side to side on its suspension. At last there was an iron groan from the bowels of the creature. It took several seconds for the last drops of pace to be strangled out of the train. When this was done there came the sound of gunfire made by the slamming doors, one of them Boychester's. The train gave out a final wheeze and started clicking.

"Dreadful thing," said Boychester, walking wide of it on the platform. He passed through the turnstile then across to the British Rail section of the station. He walked over the footbridge onto Platform One just as an Indian voice was reeling off the place names of his route: "Staines, Egham, Virginia Water, Chertsey, Addlestone, Weybridge." It sounded like a menu.

Almost at once the train arrived. No sooner had Boychester settled in opposite a man in pin-stripes than they were out over the river again, looking back up at the little mount of Richmond Hill, prettily stacked up with trees and painted terraces, and topped with the inverted cornet shape of a spire.

In ten minutes they were at the ribbon development that stalked the line. Beyond were the nameless areas of reservoir, light industry and airport. The spring in Boychester unwound still further as the gaps between the stations lengthened and farmland came in sustained bursts. There were even old, free-standing buildings in the landscape, barns and farmhouses which had shared in the organic development of the countryside; not at all like the monsters appearing in the city.

Weybridge gathered in from the edges and the train began braking. First the Wates developments and then the more solid houses at the core, and an office block still only half-tenanted despite the efforts of the location bureau.

Now Boychester could recognise the beige parental

Range Rover in the car park. It wasn't just the mother-in-law who was getting out, but Mrs. Boychester as well. She was wearing hectares of crimson cotton, free-falling from the shoulders. George had spied his father through the train window and was wincing.

Mrs. Boychester opened her arms wide with joy, like a pair of cymbals. In the middle of her freckled face the words were shaping unmistakably: "Clever Boychy!"

While Boychester was expanding in Weybridge, Cathal was contracting in The Trenches. He was on his bed – *lion couchant*. It was Saturday and he had given up on the blistering afternoon. Mr. Parnell too was hiding under the straw. From upstairs Camina's flute was coming through in wisps, rattling the pipes at every E.

There was a knock at the front door. Cathal dragged himself up and opened the window at the bedside. He peered down over the flaking cornice, expecting to see another of the Middle Eastern callers that came periodically on urgent business for one of the ghosts.

Below on the front step was the top of a dark head with slightly greased hair, tidily parted. If Cathal didn't go down the knocking would continue. That was always the way. He levered himself off the bed and padded out across the bubbly lino and down into the hall. He opened the door, ready to go through the usual disowning of whatever sin of omission had brought the caller.

The man on the step was about Cathal's height and looked self-consciously dressed in civilian clothes. He was peering sideways at Cathal, in a way that was more piercing than a straight gaze.

"Mr. Dwyer?"

The man cocked his head up with the inflection. He had a briefcase in one hand, and in the other a small plastic wallet which he flicked open and shut. Cathal didn't look down at it. He didn't need to. The officer's face was basically boyish and handsome but it had a softness about the edges that was giving away the middle-ageing process. There was something nauseating about the false tact that the features were trying to give out in the wake of the "Mr. Dwyer?"

"I am Mr. Dwyer."

The policeman muttered a rank and name and station to corroborate the card, which was back in his pocket, but the mantra went straight through Cathal.

"Pleasant enough afternoon if you like the heat," he continued, to keep the initiative, and then, after a pause: "Small matter of . . . err."

"I had forgotten it was today," said Cathal. "The appointment and that."

"Well, frankly, Mr. Dwyer, there's not a great deal to be gained from dragging one's heels about this sort of thing. Best get it over soonest. Can get very sort of blown up and dragged out."

"Quite."

"May I . . . err." He was looking past Cathal's shoulder into the dark hall and had one foot up on the step.

"Yes of course," said the Irishman, and drew aside to let him in. They walked back past the table in silence, Cathal leading. As he turned to climb the stairs he could see his caller casting a professional eye at the letters on the table. He had stopped and was fingering through some of the official-looking ones. Cathal wondered what special scraps of damning evidence this man could be gleaning with his trained eye.

"Busy days for the postman, I see," he said with a chuckle.

Cathal said warily: "Yes. Er, some are old."

"So I see. Brother Patel has a fullish in-tray, I note. Not been around recently, has he?"

Perhaps this policeman had something on the unknown Mr. Patel. Perhaps having his letters here made Cathal and Camina accessories.

"Not known here?" said the caller again with that same prying inflection, and another sideways glance up to the step where Cathal had paused.

"That's correct. Not known here. Nor many of the others."

"Mmm," said the policeman. "Ah well." They climbed the stairs, with the lower figure casting his gaze all over the walls and ceiling. Just above him one of the pipes was convulsing with an E. Cathal walked ahead across the landing and into his room. Hurriedly he gave the bedspread a yank to smooth it down as best he could and kicked the scatter of shoes and socks out of sight underneath. The policeman followed him in, still gazing around and above. He refrained from making one of his usual platitudes on such occasions, to the effect of "Nice place you've got here." Instead he went to the cage and made a sort of cheeping noise that you would to a budgie. It was a foreign tongue to Mr. Parnell, who scurried back to the wall.

Then the policeman perched at the very foot of the bed, the only sitting place he could find in this cell, and Cathal did the same up by the pillow end.

The officer was clicking his briefcase open and resuming that cruel diplomatic expression. His eyes had a guilty and shifty look; a homosexual, thought Cathal.

Eventually he said with a sigh: "Ah well, to business I suppose. You know what I mean, I expect?"

"I had a letter from your people."

"Mmm." The noise had a mock depression, as if to say: "Yes, they will write these letters, my people. Shame, but there you are."

What he actually said was: "June 15th as I understand."

"If that's what you've got."

"A Saturday?"

"I believe so."

"In the morning?"

"In the morning."

"Mmm." He was scribbling some notes in longhand on a pad over the printed sheet which looked the same as the one Cathal had got in the mail.

"Matter of a . . ."

"Pair of nuns," said Cathal.

"Well, actually more of a, what shall we say, er . . ."

"Bared arse."

The policeman giggled nervously and was definitely blushing. Then he said: "Ooo, well, Mr. Dwyer. I didn't quite say that, now did I?"

"You didn't. I did."

"Naked er . . . yes, that sort of thing."

"I shall be done for it, officer, no?"

The caller's next "Mmm" had a little interrogative upturn at the end of it. It could have meant anything—"Come again," "Aren't we being a little premature?" or even "This wretched machinery takes some stopping." What it did not contain was any hint of denial of what Cathal had just said.

"I don't know whether you want to say anything about it," the policeman began again, more officially.

"You mean a statement?"

"Mmm. Sort of."

"You want a sort of statement from me."

The policeman had gone distant now, with his pen poised over the pad, as if he just might commit to it anything of interest that happened to come up in conversation. Not that he was prying, of course.

Cathal put his hands on his knees, with stiff arms that pushed his back upright. He breathed deeply and looked downwards. He felt that familiar fury screaming up at him from his belly. But it was fury at himself and at this absurd pass. The bile he could bleed on the subject was past calculation. Except that here, with this soft-rimmed queer sitting just down the bed from him, asking him about his bare arse and presumably knowing about what he had said to the nuns better than Cathal himself, yes and knowing about the pants over the trousers, he felt impotent. He thought, naturally, of Maire and the Chairmen, where he could be as eloquent as Shaw himself on the law and the church. But for the moment he was neutered and shamed. Just like the whole Hubbard business, he was in the wrong place. He felt the little room more cell-like than ever. The man down the bed was reminding him of another unwelcome caller he had had years ago, in Wolverhampton wasn't it, while working for the *Star*; a life insurance salesman. That gentleman too had arrived at the door knowing much classified information about Cathal, presumably got from some colleague on the paper in the way that happens when reasonable men try to get such tenacious, commission-only salesmen off their own backs. He too had had this confidential manner, this way of appearing to shake hands with your heart when all the time having only your worst interests in mind. Leeches, the lot of them, licensed to dabble in your very diary or letters home.

This one was worse though, a confidant with a dagger in his jacket. It was also clear that he was getting a frisson of pleasure from the fruits of this peculiar extortionism.

"Perhaps I can help, Mr. Dwyer," he said in his sympathetic voice.

"How help? With respect, it's not your job."

"I mean help you to . . ."

"To formulate my sort of statement."

"Now, the two sisters . . ." He leafed through his papers.

"From St. Brendan's around the corner, no?"

"It hardly concerns us."

"OK, you've not denied it." Cathal's voice was low and exasperated.

"Come come, Mr. Dwyer. It's really not the end of the world, you know. Why, in my line of country I've seen far more trying little episodes than this. My word, yes. Golly, when I think of it."

He gave an effeminate cough through the circle of his thumb and forefinger. As Cathal looked at him down the bed he was filled with disgust at the thought of this devious asp getting into a police uniform just like those worn by the bonier, more masculine men in his division – the husbands and fathers among them. He pictured the sidelong glances in some police locker room or shower.

Cathal determined not to seem dejected. The more down he looked the more the officer would revel in the confessor role.

"Look, it's like this, officer," he said. "That morning, whenever it was, I . . . well, I just went downstairs, that's all."

"Not quite all, it would appear. According to the sisters . . ."

"Will you leave them out. Just for a moment. Please. I just went downstairs. Now then, it happens that on that day the paper boy – and they're a lax bunch round here – couldn't be bothered to get the papers half way up the step. So, in a word, I went down after them."

"And you were at the time . . ."

"Hell, yes, you know I was, man. Not a stitch."

"Mmm. And was your . . . you know . . . showing. The other side? Mmm?"

"Lord no. I was on my belly at the time."

"Mmm. There is something that you possibly said to the . . . er sisters . . . about, let me see, ah yes, a worm and a pyramid. Could that be it?"

The policeman was trying to sound incredulous, as if witnesses were such pedantic creatures.

"Damn'd if I know. Really officer. I do not know."

"And then I understand there was something to do with a pair of underpants."

"I had a headache in the morning."

The policeman wrote out "headache" painstakingly.

"I was not feeling well."

"Been celebrating, eh?"

Again the sideways glance.

"I do not see that it is relevant."

"Just my little joke, Mr. Dwyer. Just my little joke."

"I was not feeling well. Look, I had had some trouble with my clothes."

"Mmm. Yes. They can be tricky things . . ."

"Now they can't touch me for that, can they?"

"Touch you, Mr. Dwyer?"

"You know. It's not an offence."

"Not my line, I'm afraid. Can't be sure what is and what is not an offence these days. That's up to the beaks."

"So I will be up at the magistrates."

"Really, Mr. Dwyer. Don't jump to all these conclusions. I simply said that it is the beaks who decide these things."

The word "beak" came oddly from the policeman. It was a careful token of an irreverence that did not exist.

"I'm not jumping, officer. But you know the game as well as I do. What do you reckon then?"

"Reckon?"

"You know. A fine."

"I'm afraid you really are running ahead, Mr. Dwyer. Now, do you wish me to know anything more?"

"Officer, I'm not denying anything. Not anything. They can say whatever they like. You can tell them that. I'll wear it. I'll put my name to it."

The policeman was putting his papers back into the briefcase, which Cathal noticed had two faded initials, J. G., embossed on the side. He felt another pang of nausea at this personal evidence showing, the salesman again. It seemed grotesque to have his own degrading papers in that case which must at some time have carried J. G.'s own correspondence with friends, or banks, or insurance companies. What a way to cross paths with a professional stranger.

Both of them standing now, Cathal looked him in the face and said: "Well, I expect I'll be hearing from you again soon, then?"

This time the "mmm" was accompanied by a hangdog look that tried to mean: "Yes, I suppose so. A drag, but there you are. The whole process just goes on like a juggernaut."

"Mmm," he said again. "From my people."

"Well, you'll forgive me if I don't thank you for calling," said Cathal with a little more dignity.

"Oh, quite. Quite."

They both stood looking at the door.

"I'll find my own way out," said the policeman. Before leaving he walked over to Mr. Parnell's cage again and made the same cheeping noise as before. Then, almost jauntily, he said "By-ee" into the space between the hamster and its master, and was gone.

Back on his bed Cathal imagined the guilty salesman picking his way down the scene of the crime and out through the empty gateway, briefcase in hand.

Mr. Parnell had also lost his innocence. He was a budgie manqué and the thought of it trammelled his freedom of movement. He thought to himself: "I am wingless," and moped.

Down on the pavement the policeman looked back at the path, puzzled like all the visitors by the cleanliness of it. Knowing that Cathal would be at the first floor window, he didn't look up, but passed on down the way of the nuns.

"Well, what do you reckon then, Mr. Parnell?" said Cathal. "Up at the beak's for a bare bum, what? Mrs. Weekes will be there no doubt, drama critic at life's theatre." The show might even be graced by a royal progress in the form of Boychester. And why not the new Sizer too, and Hubbard and the rest of the skeletons. A show of retribution would not be lost on them. Just like the old times. Tyburn and everything.

Many a true word in jest. As he pattered on at Mr. Parnell, the reality of this possibility came home to him. After all, if there was a summons – and the policeman's visit had done nothing to ease the fears planted by his people's letter – then Cathal would be standing on the very spot of magistrate's floor where so many others had been turned to Pinkies.

It was an appalling thought. He had had it before, standing in the hall with the letter in his hand and wondering what the gloating relatives would say to see the story in the Irish papers. But all that had been a fantasy conceived in shock, a sort of safety device to pre-empt the worst. Now the fantasy did not look so wild. He could picture Boychester saying to Mrs. Weekes when the case came up: "After all, it is in our patch, is it not. Right in it, and the defendant is local moreover." He could also see him adding self-righteously: "We have a duty to inform our public, even if the matter is as painfully near home as this." To think that only the other day Cathal was actually planning to involve Mrs. Weekes in the whole matter, to seek her advice. Better give matches to an arsonist. Mrs. Weekes would sharpen her pencil for court and etch her pad with the usual prurience. There would be no favours done for him. The random censorship of absence would be withheld by the growing Boychester/Weekes alliance.

Boychester would articulate what Mrs. Weekes would be thinking. It would run like this: "If a man should distinguish himself, we will honour him. If however he should command public attention for reasons that might be ignoble, then shall he likewise get it, regardless of station or standing."

Cathal supplied the Boychester drift in this way until the dreadful plausibility of it made him want to stop. If he could have sustained such a flow in another direction, "The Partition" would by now have been in repertory in a dozen cities. But what he could not have guessed as he sat on the bed plotting out his own aggressor's campaign was the chilling accuracy of the prophecy.

"And how long have you been with the paper, David Camina?"

"About s – six months."

"About? About six months? What is this word 'about' ?"

"My starting date will be in your files."

"My starting date will be in your files, indeed. I ask for information and am given a reference to my own sources. This is very singular."

"I – I think I started in December, just before Christmas."

"I am aware that the bulk of December is just before Christmas. Not, however, all of it. Some precision please."

"I think it was the second Monday."

"The second Monday, Mr. Boychester, sir. Well?"

"The second Monday, Mr. Boychester sir."

"That's better. Now then, what was the first thing you learned here?"

"I don't know what you want me to say. Mr. Boychester sir."

"I don't want you to say what you think I might want to hear. For a start you would in all probability be wrong. Now then, think."

"It was that when out on a job for the paper, I represent the paper."

"So you do have a memory?"

Camina was silent.

"And do you think that the paper is best represented at an important function by a spotty youth in jeans and plimsoles, and with no tie?"

"I – I can't help . . ."

"You can't help the spots, don't tell me. These things happen at your age. No doubt your mother invested a fortune in an unblemished skin for you."

"I know about the spots. I had them when you interviewed me."

"But the plimsoles, David Camina. Symptoms of physical immaturity as well? I think not."

"Clothes are very expensive, and the Newspaper Society . . ."

"The Newspaper Society, eh? And what does David Camina know of the Newspaper Society?"

"I know that it was founded last century by publishers objecting to taxation imposed by the Government on advertising revenue."

"We have an historian among us! A little A. J. P. Camina!"

"You asked me."

"Do not answer back."

Boychester, at one end of the newsroom, looked past Camina to where Cathal, Pam, Harvey and Mrs. Weekes were working in a strained silence.

"You were about to say that the Newspaper Society pays you a wage low enough to keep your back shirtless. No?"

"Not exactly, Mr. Boychester."

"In my young days the need for husbandry was considered a good training, a perk of the job."

Cathal thought with disgust of the new style to which a good marriage had accustomed Boychester.

"I am not a cold man, David Camina, nor am I where I am today through coldness. But yesterday at Rotary – I was ashamed. Ashamed that there now appears to be room for scruffs in this great profession. As a brilliant young theorist with wit and literacy your prose should of course be gracing the columns of the *New Statesman* or indeed (he said this with archness and contempt) . . . or indeed the *London Jewish Quarterly*. Meanwhile you are doomed to slum it with the *Bugle*. Or is it the other way round?"

"I don't quite understand."

"Are we doomed to slum it with you?"

Here Boychester strode in a circle round his patch of floor, head bowed, arms behind his back in the Royalty position. He looked like a great pigeon thinking about mating. Below the dirty window children were at play in the memorial garden, and Camina wished he could have been one of them.

Boychester completed another circle and, facing Camina, said: "Many would have relished the chance of being sent out on the front lead."

The other four faces in the room looked incredulous, but Boychester didn't notice them.

"The front lead, Camina. A major statement on press freedom, at an important local assembly, by a not unknown figure."

At each of the three points he stabbed the air with a folded piece of paper he had just taken from his pocket.

"And the assignment goes, not to a tired veteran such as Mrs. Weekes (she preened slightly but pretended not to have heard), but to one D. Camina, junior. My policy of encouraging youth through early challenges is not something you find on every newspaper, good gracious no."

Early challenges, thought Camina. Yesterday, while he had been forking his way through the thin diarrhoea and maggots of which Cathal had warned, Boychester had been swelling like a toad on the top table, still undeflated after three days back from Weybridge. Occasionally he had looked down to where Camina was seated, near the door from which clanging trolleys and the clatter of crockery would emerge.

Boychester had looked more than ever like the sergeant on the bridge, and for a few dangerous moments Camina had felt himself being pulled towards the edge of sleep. He could remember being aware of Boychester looking blackly at him from the table.

Now the editor was saying: "Your note, David Camina. If you please." He held out his right hand and looked away from Camina towards the window, like a butler with a tray.

Camina walked round to his desk and picked up a tatty spiral-bound pad. He started leafing through it for the page which would say "B'chstr" at the top. For what seemed like an eternity he thumbed through the half-empty pages, many of which had lines of verse or sketches of gaunt faces.

Still frozen in his waiting position, Boychester said impatiently: "Give it to me please. I wish to view it."

Camina handed it over and there was another very long silence. He began leafing.

"Not just an historian, I see," said Boychester. "But also an artist. And a poet to boot. A war poet, no less. Well well."

On the page with "B'chstr" at the top there was a line drawing clearly showing a man standing in the middle of a row of seated diners. One of them was unmistakable as the Rotary branch secretary, a large balding head with a cruel slit of a mouth. The speaker's face was an exaggerated circle, and round the badge on his lapel were the stylised rays of a picture-book sun. There was an arrow pointing to the midriff from the margin, where the words "sow-suit" were written. There was also a bubble coming from the mouth, containing the words "Blah blah blah blah blah."

From the corner of an eye Cathal at his desk saw Boychester's eyebrows rise. Maire was strongly in his thoughts. He was in the wrong place again. He picked up his phone and began to dial a number, in the hope of relieving the tension.

But Boychester, the still-expanded son-in-law, the man with a future and a direct line to the power base, was above belittlement. Besides, he nurtured no illusions about his esteem in this quarter, not since certain discoveries. Camina's defeated look told him that aggression was superfluous.

"In my day," he said, "I was told that a picture was worth a thousand words. You, David Camina, are of the same school, I conclude. I see the picture, but I find no evidence of a thousand words with which to compare it. Perhaps you can help me here."

"There are notes on the next page."

Boychester turned the page. He examined the scrawl and said: "You will forgive my naivety. An historian I am not. An artist I am not. A war poet I am certainly not. And yet . . . and yet, my simple man's memory tells me that yesterday what I said at Rotary was this . . ." (In his left hand he held up the transcript.) "Now am I to be persuaded that what I really said was . . . this?" (In the right he held Camina's notebook.) "As a gentleman of the press, one of the old school, you can explain for me this slight discrepancy."

"I – I didn't think it was all important."

"I have told you. It is to be the lead. The front page lead. The story beneath the masthead. By David Camina."

"I did not know it was so important."

"Well, we shall hear what David Camina considers important on matters relating to the freedom of the press. Read, if you would."

He handed the notebook back to Camina, whose combination of a stammer and a totally inadequate note reduced the Boychester oratory to something like this: "A l-lot of n-nonsense has been talked about p-press freedom."

Boychester was comparing it with the typed sheet from which he had spoken.

"Wh-what are we to think wh-when, no, if, if printers gladly handle type condemning Conservative policies and then . . . and then strike over reports showing their own union's executive in a self-seeking light?"

There was another silence.

"Go on, please," said Boychester.

"I – I can recall a time when . . ."

"You have left out 800 words."

Camina felt like a schoolboy trying to fudge a Latin unseen.

"Where are my 800 words? I would like to know what they were. Have they simply gone? Since yesterday?"

"You have them in your hand."

"As it happens, I do. But what if I didn't? What if I had destroyed them after use, as would have been my inalienable right? Is the public to be given that, that travesty as my speech? Well?"

The children in the memorial garden let out a high screech as their ball went under the legs of the tramps on the bench.

"I will have the notebook back, thank you," said Boychester. "Your colleagues will have formed their own opinions of your work. Meanwhile, there are others with whom I must liaise on the standard of trainees within this group. It is a task which demeans us all, not least myself, but one from which I shall not shrink. The notebook please. Thank you."

V
Last Orders

BOBSY MARSHALL GOSHED in disbelief as her lover drove hard into her again. She was splayed in submission underneath. The borough was autumnal now, and the pavements of the luckier parts were rusty with leaves; but Bobsy was blooming in Brondesbury. For the summer she had been as bored as a bricked up tunnel while her husband struck usurious bargains with his bright pills in Guinea-Bissau. She had delivered 13,800 leaflets, collected 3,000 petition forms and attended 59 meetings of 18 committees.

But dogs still defaecated on the pavement. One was doing so now, outside Bobsy's house. It was a tatty little mongrel, and he squatted defiantly in the text book pose, as if he knew who lived inside. Even if Bobsy had been aware of him, she would have waived her militancy at this moment. Her chin was forced sharply back by the shoulder that banged it with every thrust from below. The lover's head was buried in the pillow and he was grunting rhythmically. The ceiling swam above her and her whimpers climbed into a long squeal which she tried to interrupt with: "Oh yes, yes. How you love me. Oh."

After the stiffness that followed and gave these two slack bodies a rigidity they had never known, they softened into each other with a sigh and the moist paunches melted back into the No Man's Land of flesh between them. Over the shoulder, which was heavy now, she could see the flat buttocks at rest in the V of her thighs. A trail of clothes had been abandoned between the bed and the couch where the petting had started. On the floor were strewn the last and smallest garments which had been flung there as it became obvious that the kissing could have only one conclusion.

The man's body was as still as death, and he appeared to have stopped breathing. Even his recoiling part had suspended the withdrawal. Bobsy's first thought was that he was dead. With all the strength she could muster she wriggled to her right and half dumped, half slid the bulk onto the sheet beside her like a beached whale. Everything from the head to the organ, glistening and still heavy with blood, mirrored the downward thrust of the man, horizontally as vertically.

He wasn't dead, but spent after this unaccustomed exercise and a heavy intake of house red with Charles ffitch. He came to with a greedy snort.

"Oh Boychester," said Bobsy, "you are wonderful. My delicious, wonderful lover. What a man."

"Why, my thanks to you."

"Oh no. Mine. My thanks."

She lay back radiantly on the pillow and prepared to talk. The port after the dinner.

"My husband doesn't understand me."

She was wrong there. He understood her very well, which was why he was even now travelling the Dark Continent with a bagful of samples, maybe pausing in a Mombasa bar to fantasise about a swift but terminal illness for her.

Boychester didn't want the port, nor the hand that reached out for his beading hair to claim a new intimacy beyond the pubic zones. Already the lunch hangover was biting. He felt moody and aggressive. He would get out with the minimum fuss. Her intimate smells and her very presence next to him in place of Mrs. Boychester disgusted him. Damn the husband who didn't understand her. What was there to be understood anyway?

Boychester's taking of a lover in this unlovely shape was not the only development in the three months just passed since the week of the Rotary lead.

Just round the corner from where the stud now swung his body from the love bed, Larch Towers was burgeoning on like a tree defying the seasons. The sap that had been rising in the spring was rising still. The flowering cherry was long out of flower and arched back even more incredulously at the art rooms that were taking shape above the gables and vying with the turret for height. The builders were finishing their work so quickly that only a week or two of the Christmas term would be disrupted.

Across the street from the school Mrs. Boychester was pregnant again, though it was difficult to see how she could get any larger.

There was a new set of silent and haunted faces coming and going from the other bedsits in The Trenches. One, a very thin man with a jaw that looked plastic in the half-light, had stayed for four days and was only remembered by the menacing letters that poured in for him after he had gone.

The postman delivering to The Trenches noticed how dull the tiles on the front path had become as he fed Cathal's summons, heavy as a mortar shell, into the hall.

As for Flaherty, or the part of him jailed in the sow-suit,

he had been liquidated in the pocket of the garment, which Boychester had taken to the cleaners to make it shine afresh for the autumn. It must have been a terrible death for Flaherty. He had come out still in the same pocket, but thin as a wafer and washed clean of words, like a man just dead from hunger strike.

Camina had been dreaming ever more violently since the last brush with Boychester. As Isaac Rosenberg he had been pinioned with leather thongs to the top of a large trolley like the one at the Rotary. The exhausted corporal had been on the lower deck and the thing had been rolled by the two men in mufti down a ramp into the mud below the duckboards. There, before waking, he had felt the back of his head clash against a jaw-bone under the surface.

Then there was the island site, *Bugle* and all. In the elbow of Fountain Street the memorial garden, the jumped-up workhouse of a building, and the Chairmen still stood. But in the council's planning offices a few miles away were rolls of sheets with meticulous ink lines allocating down to the last millimetre the air that would soon be hanging over the site. The battle, if it could be called that, to save the old *Bugle* works had been lost. A self-loving little conservation group (Hon. Treas. Bobsy Marshall) had trotted out all the drab incantations of Heritage, Changing Face, People Before Profit, and at a public meeting attended by 10 people she had made a fool of herself by talking about the 18th century façade of the building.

As she had never been to the works it was understandable that she should get them muddled with the register office. A far larger body of opinion favoured the complex of supermarket and multi-storey car park that was to replace the works around a slightly reduced memorial garden.

The *Bugle* itself and its passionate leader-writer were strangely silent about the whole thing. Given that the very owners of the building were eager to see it turned to rubble, for a price, this again was understandable. Mrs. Weekes of course had shed tears for the fate of the building, which was something she never managed to do for sentenced humans. Her sorrow could have had something to do with the fact that this place had for so long pulped out her Pinkies for display. It was a warehouse of retribution that could never be properly replaced by new plant. In the next regime, imminent now, it would all seem so clean and innocent compared with the mediaeval grindings of the metal beast.

Her tears were kept from Boychester, with whom her hopes of preferment in the strange country of Holborn rested as surely as his did with Sturridge. After all, this was the one-but-last week.

Just like other spare parts, linotype men were hard to come by now. The pall of smoke over the glass enclosure was thinner, and you could locate the operators by the individual puffs that rose above them. Most of the young ones had either left or were on the re-training course in Holborn. Like the Coming Men they were entranced by the power and potential of the screen and the little white army locked inside to wait for the marching orders of the fingers.

The oars of the static regatta were moving up and down with the abandon of a defeated crew. Most of the typesetting was outwork these days, sent down to a printer in Epsom or Ewell. The metal slugs, in all manner of different faces, came back late on press days to be slotted in on the formes with the rest of the type by the depleted compositors.

More and more strange men in suits came round, and the West Indian carding the impurities from the molten lead didn't bother to look up any more. The men would point in great arcs around the skylights and the arrangement of rods and ratchets that opened them. They would walk past the stone with looks of faint disgust, and then move in parties through the rubber doors and down into the bowels, where they would still try to talk against the roar.

For the *Bugle* itself, next week was to be the last in hot metal. With a speed rare in this industry Hubbard had struck in the height of summer. People had returned from their holidays to find terse memos detailing the *fait accompli*. For a short time it had looked as though the tidal wave of progress would break messily, with all sorts of debris showing through as the water settled; but that was before Hubbard bought out certain of the printers with redundancy payments so generous that it was assumed he had finally lolled into senility. In fact his ancestors looked down approvingly at the green table in Holborn where he was ticking on like a perfect watch to a late hour.

He had conquered his shock over new technology – with a little help from Sturridge – and the two men now went regularly to trade exhibitions all over the country. Hubbard was even getting a reputation for lobbing the most awkward questions at the thrusting young men on the stands.

The old Sizer, with sugar basin and ash tray on the lunch table, had not been entirely wrong about the future. As from the week after next the *Bugle* would indeed be based in Holborn, with Boychester still in charge – for the moment – and still with his full complement of staff – for the moment. After that, well, there were dark rumours that Boychester's empire would be slashed to a single page, a slip edition of the main group. This had reached the editor via Mrs. Weekes, and he, outwardly at least, discounted it. The *Bugle*, he argued, was the prestige publication carrying the banner ahead of the field into the promised land. A wider belief was that Boychester's organ had no rival as cannon-fodder for this hazardous venture.

Even now, as his image flashed back full-length at him from Bobsy's wardrobe mirror, the words "slip edition" entered his head, together with the refrain that had haunted him on the train. For a second he thought he saw his trunk narrowed to the same spindliness as his legs.

One thing, to use his language, was certain: all eyes would be on Boychester's *Bugle* next week as an era ended. He dressed hurriedly, and the first words of his "Message to our Readers" were forming.

In Berkshire Hubbard himself was well pleased with the deal. The old presses in the bowels of the works were still good for another year, until the redevelopment, and after that the group would contract out to a plant in Uxbridge. It was all arranged. Even old Tom in Sunningdale liked the wheeze and celebrated with a winning streak at the bowling club. He called his chairman "a first rate groundsman" and there was no higher praise than that.

But Mr. Parnell was out of sorts, and the wheel was silent. He had either seen the summons or guessed that life on Boychester's coat-tails at this time was no life for his master.

Oddly enough the Chairmen, which had always been ready to slide off the island at any minute, had won a reprieve. This was not due to Bobsy Marshall, who had not noticed the "distinctive arched windows and panelling" which had won the building a right to life from the Department of the Environment.

Another unlikely survivor, the little train, had had a good summer as well, and found itself on the tube maps. And this without Boychester's support.

The editor took his tie from the expensive new Xerox machine in Bobsy's bedroom and finished dressing. She was still lying on the bed, looking at him mistily as he moved about the room to gather the last of his clothes. His movements became more and more frenetic. He sat on a chair and bent down to tie his shoes. He looked at his watch and gasped. Suddenly he was on his feet again, striding across to the door. He paused there to say "Goodbye then," and clumped down the stairs almost loudly enough to miss the beginnings of the long weep seeping from the room.

The mongrel outside was answering another call of nature further down the pavement. Boychester felt disgusted by the quivering of the furry haunches. As he pulled his tie straight and looked away, a voice from the other direction said: "Boychy! Coming home so soon! Jogger. Look!" Mrs. B., gleaming in the autumn light, was walking the little man along the kerb. As she stopped, the tiny knuckle of her pregnancy showed through the drapery. George went silent and Boychester said: "Good afternoon to you. Mrs. Marshall – she of the association – wanted my advice. I could not refuse it."

"Kind Boychy," she said. "Clever, kind Boychy," and put his arm through hers.

"So it would appear that my arse is a matter of legitimate public concern, Camina," said Cathal in the Chairmen.

It was Monday, the first day of the last week, opening time in the evening, and Cathal due in court the next morning. But not in a professional capacity. That job had gone to who else but Mrs. Weekes.

"You know, Camina, I never thought I would have such greatness thrust upon me. By my own organ, if you follow me."

"Boychester is a cunt," said Camina.

"There you libel cunts."

"Last week then, Cathal," said Maire at the optic. "Shame, now. Off to Holborn, then?"

"Aye. And I don't fancy the idea myself. Why it's all full of lawyers with briefcases, and pubs you can't get into at lunchtime, and sandwiches that cost £2."

"That's right, Cathal. Not a nice place like round here."

"I shall be in Saturdays."

"Course you will. And the odd evening as well if I know you."

"Perhaps."

"So you're going over to the televisions, I've heard."

"We are."

"You don't like them if I remember."

"I don't."

"They're the things as the maggots get lost in and make your knees go numb, aren't they?"

Cathal managed to chuckle. "Yes, Maire. It's a fair description."

"And I thought no-one was going to use them because of their being anti-social and that. I read it in the papers. They give you cancer or schizophrenia or something."

"Both probably."

"And I read that no-one was going to touch them

no-how, being as they're craftsmen or guildsmen and that all this new stuff was going rusty."

"They weren't, my love. But money talks, and old man Hubbard's been shouting with it. £20,000 for stopping work. It's more than I'll see in years and years."

"There's no justice, Cathal."

"Right enough."

"And the works is to come down, no?"

"Every bit of it. In a year or so. You're safe though."

"So it says in the *Bugle*. Little piece on the back page. Mick's glad. But he says he can't think what they see in the windows and the panels. Says they're good enough for being sick against and that they wipe down easy and that's all. He was planning to get rid of them and put up something less, you know, fussy like, when he does the partition."

While she was speaking Cathal had fallen into a reverie, thinking of the next morning and wondering whether to tell Maire that his arse was to be preserved in metal. When she said "partition" he looked up sharply.

"There is to be a partition?"

"Yes. Where you're standing. Can't see the point of it myself, but Mick says that we've got two sorts of customers and that they should have different areas. He's been counting them and putting little numbers on a piece of paper in his back room."

"Flaherty would be tickled."

"Who, Cathal?"

"Oh, a friend of mine. Never mind."

At that moment Joan and Wheeler came in. She sat down and he walked to the bar, hunched up in his bum-freezer. The two were clearly courting now and they seemed to take a pleasure in being seen in a place so far below the dignity of their calling. Perhaps they wanted to keep themselves secret from council colleagues, but more probably they had heard, again from Mrs. Weekes, of tomorrow's court appearance and were hoping to stare at the guilty man before he mounted the tumbril. Both looked satisfied and unafraid on finding him here. Wheeler and Cathal were standing on either side of the invisible partition.

"Evening, House Plant," said Cathal. But there was no triumph in his voice.

"Good evening, Mr. Dwyer," said Wheeler. Then to Maire: "Two gins and one tonic if you would." Then to Cathal again: "Interesting week? News-wise?"

Joan smiled smugly in the corner. She smoothed down her pleated skirt, crossed her legs, and took from her handbag a long cigarette with a gold band round the filter.

"Fascinating," answered Cathal. "But not a great deal with a gas angle, I'm afraid."

Before sitting down with Joan, Wheeler put a record on the juke box so that they could talk unheard. It was the confounded "Thousands Are Sailing." Cathal flinched, and wished for a partition. He resumed his conversation with Maire.

"So the Chairmen will be tucked under the new slab?"

"It will, I suppose."

"And what do you think of that?"

"Oh, it's a job, Cathal."

"And what does Mick think?"

"Mick says it's better than having the brewery shunt him off somewhere or else give him the bullet altogether."

"You'll not get much trade when you're in a heap of rubble."

"No, but the brewery is seeing him all right, he says.

And they reckon it'll pick up even better when the shopping goes up."

"Probably will. Probably will."

Mick came through from the back of the pub and let out a colossal fart which made him grunt from the other end in pain and relief. He hitched his belt up on the underside of his belly, and it fell down again.

"Evening, Cathal," he said. "Sorry to hear about the court business."

"Aye," said Cathal. "Church and the law got me between them. Not the first time. Won't be the last."

Maire showed no surprise.

"I've some poteen," Mick whispered. "Will you try a drop?"

"I will."

"It's on me."

"Bless you."

"Celebrating, oh I don't know what. Lots of things. And drowning a few more."

From under the bar he brought up a bottle of clear white liquid. As if to prove his own muscle in arm-wrestling he poured a drop onto the bar and then lit the little puddle with a match. A flame rose from it, clear and orange at the top. Almost as quickly it guttered and died.

Mick grunted in satisfaction and passed a wet rag across the bar. From the middle of the damp patch a spot the size of the poteen puddle dried before the water and became a little island.

"There now," said Mick. "Sort of fights back, doesn't it."

He poured two glasses and, just before putting the cork back, a third for Camina. Mick lifted his glass and said: "To fighting back, then."

The three of them drank, and as the liquid went down,

grimaced in an agony of pleasure. Maire looked from one to the other, an experienced referee in these things. Cathal felt the drink reach into his fingers and toes. Then he said: "To the Chairmen. Long may it stand. Undivided."

There was hostility in the last word.

"You've heard of the partition plan then, Cathal?" said the landlord.

"I have." He was already affected too much by the drink to think of the project in any other terms than Flaherty's.

"And you don't like it," said Mick.

"Not a lot."

"Well then we'll drink to the melting of the maggot televisions in Holborn and the downfall of Barchester."

"That will come," said Camina with a sudden firmness. "That will come for certain."

"The lad sounds mighty sure," said Mick.

"He does," said Cathal. "I cannot share his hopes. Boychester is on the up, which is why I'm on the down and in the dock."

"Boychester will get what he deserves, and sooner than you know," said Camina again, with the clarity of someone else's voice.

"Well then another one to Barchester's come-uppance as it's such a certain thing," said Mick and they drank.

After he had unclenched himself from the swallow, Cathal said: "Boychester is in the pink, Camina. He is making ready for Sizer's Holborn in grand order."

"Is Sizer the maggot man?" asked Maire.

"He is, dear. The midwife, sort of. And Boychester's been courting him mightily. So when all the televisions are in full swing and the whole thing's as neat as a pocket handkerchief and the *Bugle* gets sucked up as a slip like a fleck of snot, Boychester will be all right."

Maire was puzzled by this business of slips and handkerchiefs, but she said "oh" gamely.

Cathal went on: "Me and Camina, though: we're hostages to fortune. Him because he nods off at Rotary in mid-Boychester, and me because I, well, you'll see that in the last metal *Bugle.*"

"What's the last metal *Bugle?*" asked Maire.

"The last one before the televisions come on," the landlord supplied.

"And is it true what they're saying, you know, about the nuns?" Maire asked again.

"Is what true?" said Cathal wearily.

"Well, about them in the street and all the things you were doing to them."

"You'd best tell me all the things I was doing to them, and then I'll let you know. Although there's a few things I could do to them now."

"Well," Maire began, "that you hid under a hedge with a stick when they passed by and lifted one of their skirts and then . . ."

Cathal interrupted her: "Is that what they're alleging, is it? Lord no, it was far worse than that. Seeing as you're broad-minded . . .". He reached across the bar and pulled her by the back of the neck into whispering distance.

Two seconds later she gasped, drew from Cathal and slapped a hand over the O of her mouth.

"I did so," Cathal confirmed.

"Why, you never."

"Yes I did."

"Well," said Mick, passing the bottle over the three glasses and spilling as much in the gaps: "We'd better drink to a lenient beak."

"I'll drink," said Cathal, with the anger rising again,

"but not to no lenient beak. Hell, I'm an Irishman and there's no such thing here for an Irishman. Anyway, I don't want no English beak's leniency. I'm a newsman, and I'll create a good story for Boychester and his *Bugle*. He'll never get one by himself."

The tune on the juke-box ended, for the third or fourth time, and the two PRs caught the end of Cathal's raised voice. The little group, two on each side of the bar, looked round furtively, like passengers caught shouting when the train stops. With something approaching vengeance in his face Wheeler took the next coin from his pile on the table and put the song on again.

"Cathal," said Mick with compassion, "you're talking a little mad. You've done nothing greatly wrong and you shouldn't let that Barchester fellow put you down. Besides, our young friend says he's for a fall, and somehow I believe him."

Cathal was drunk. He began again, slurred: "Mrs. Weekes is covering, and she'll get nothing wrong. You shall have the truth of the case from Friday's *Bugle* if you want it. Correct, Camina?"

"We shall certainly have the truth. Yes, Cathal." Then, rather cryptically: "Whatever's in the paper will be true."

Cathal went on: "One of groovy Harvey's friends at the law centre told groovy Harvey I shouldn't worry. He said something about, I don't know what, erogenous zones, I think. Said they couldn't get me without a, pardon my French, Maire – stiff prick. Perhaps and perhaps not. They're all in it together, these law fellows and they've enough clauses to make a baby pregnant. They'll do it if they want."

"You're letting it get to you, Cathal," said Mick, "which is just what your Barchester would want. Don't give him the pleasure, now. Besides, look there. Your friends from the Umpteenth Estate. They're Barchester people, aren't they?"

"They are."

"Well then." He poured another round. "We'll drink to . . ."

"To Mr. Parnell," Cathal interrupted.

"To who?" said Maire.

"Mr. Par-nell," he repeated.

"Does he come in here?"

Cathal rolled his eyes at the girl's ignorance. "No, he does not come in here, and more's the pity. He'd not have any of your partitions if he did. You wouldn't want them, neither."

"Is he in the building trade?"

"Yes dear," he sighed. "You might say that."

"We'll drink to him," said Mick, and he did.

"The hero and the hamster," said Cathal.

This was beyond Maire. She leant her elbows on the bar, lodging a fat chin in her hands, and stared a bemused stare at the nun-molester.

"Have you never learned nothing of history?" said Cathal.

"You just said he was a hamster," she giggled.

"Charles Stewart," said Mick helpfully.

She felt under pressure and said: "I thought he was a builder, the way you were talking. Is he from the town hall then?"

Cathal was preparing his description, and the comparison between Parnell and himself because of them both being brought down by women, the church and the law. But the speech was beyond him. Very deliberately he intoned "Kitty O'Shea," as if he were saying "Once Upon a

Time," and then gave up with a wave of a hand in the direction of his glass.

"Leave him alone, shall we," said Mick. "He's all in. I'm ringing for a cab."

At the realisation that he was about to be transported to The Trenches, with nothing but darkness and shame and loneliness between him and the magistrates, Cathal fought back.

"My arse is to be graven in the last ingot," he shouted. "And all you can do is send me on my way. You are staring history in the backside and trying to bung it with a cork. You will please let me be."

Mick put the receiver back on the wall phone.

"I am a celebrity in the making," Cathal went on, "and I will not be blacked out."

Wheeler took his hand off Joan's knee. He sidled it round the back of her shoulders and she leant forward compliantly. Before getting up to go to the juke box again he said to her in a voice which Camina could just catch: "It'll be better than a movie in court tomorrow. Same again – love?"

At about the same hour two figures were working late in Holborn. There was a dull glow from the one lit screen in the centre of the large room. The place smelled of fresh paint and carpet, which disguised the considerable age of the building. On all sides of the two men were more tables, similar to their own, fanning away to the walls in open plan. Each one had four screens on it, set in a cruciform, so that the operators would be looking at the rear profile of the next man's face.

Many people might have been surprised to learn that

there was room for such an emporium in Holborn, cluttered as it was with alleys and courts, and the busy litigants that teemed through them. But if they knew the area better they would have realised that all those passages which linked the roads as though only by a series of accidents were an illusion: they were cramped and crooked precisely because buildings like this one had asserted their bulk with no concession to the passer-through. There was space enough inside for Hubbard's purposes, and Sturridge's, and the outside could make its own arrangements. That had always been the way, and planning was a subversive concept.

"Wonderful. Wonderful," said Hubbard.

"Not bad, sir, is it," said Sturridge.

Outside the autumn light was fading above the strange assortment of gables across the precinct, and softened the cusps and jagged teeth below which the actions, suits and counter-claims of the day had ended. Two young clerks shared a joke and their footsteps clicked sharply away across the paving stones in opposite directions. The traffic was a dull roar all round, with occasionally a high-tuned motor sounding above the blur.

"It's everything I could have hoped for," said the old man, and pressed another key. The characters before his eyes flicked and shifted and froze into the new posture as commanded.

"I'm glad you like it, sir," said Sturridge.

"I do. I do." His fingers ranged across the keyboard again. "And am I right in thinking there are enough setters from the retraining course for the first *Bugle*?"

"Oh, absolutely, sir," said Sturridge, reaching for his file. "We've even a surplus of let me see now . . . three, four, five. A surplus of five."

"And the completion of the second training period will be in six weeks, you said?"

"Yes sir. It's bang on schedule. By that time we should have the cold type capacity for very nearly the entire group, classifieds included. Of course, it might mean some overtime initially, unless the pagination is reduced."

"Quite, quite. Well, we shall keep our options open. The pagination question will probably be solved by you-know-what."

"The *Bugle*, sir?"

"I had the Audit Bureau of Circulation figures last week. Appalling. Worse than ever. Do you know the man Boychester? Orange-faced chap?"

"A little, sir. He rings me from time to time."

"I think he was a mistake." Hubbard played with the grey-cased toy in front of him again and twinkled with delight at its obedience. "We shall see. Of course we shan't wish to carry all of them. Not in a few months."

"Of course not, sir."

Still preoccupied, the old man said: "I sometimes think I don't understand people."

"Oh?"

"I mean printers."

"Are they people, sir?"

"Now now, Sturridge. No, I don't understand these people who cling to their old ways at all costs. Pure traditionalism is not what made us great, you know."

"No sir."

"The best of the old and the best of the new. That's the formula, isn't it?"

"Of course, sir."

"To hear some of these fellows talk you'd think they'd be only too glad to get rid of that hot metal nonsense.

Ingots dangling from chains into tubs, wretched little chips of metal so hot that you can't pick them up, a stupid old machine they wouldn't touch if it was a used car. And then you give them a new option, something fresh and clean like this, and they start griping about job satisfaction. Extraordinary."

"Quite extraordinary, sir."

"That is, until the cheque-book comes out. Which it did, by God. Tell me, Sturridge. Is there anything which is not purchasable?"

"Errr . . ."

"In the way of reason, logic, emotion. Is there?"

"I wouldn't know, sir."

"See how our friend in the overalls changes his line when I reach for the wallet. Eh?"

He tapped the keys again and muttered, almost inaudibly, "Thank the Lord for property." Standing in the middle of the screen now was the single word "Bugle", little white square letters in the pool of grey. After looking at it for a couple of seconds he flushed it away with a stroke of his thumb and the screen was blank.

At the same hour in Brondesbury Boychester was carrying two glasses of Bobsy Marshall's wine into his back garden, where a canvas chair was invisible under Mrs. B. There was a hint of moisture in the air, carrying the scent of new creosote from a fence two gardens down. It was also getting into the points of a car in the street, and the flagging starting motor cooed like a wood pigeon. George was sleeping upstairs. Boychester sat down and drank a healthy swig of the wine as if it were beer. It was of very good quality, and the case must have cost Bobsy a lot. But the bouquets were stifled by being rushed across the tongue like this and straight down into the throat. The taste did have a certain significance for the drinker, not an entirely pleasant one. It took him back to the awful intimacies of Bobsy's room, where she had poured him several glasses of the same on the dressing table with her husband's photo shining up with the trust of early marriage. It also brought back to Boychester memories of the even more ghastly smell that had wafted up to his face the next time he had stood at the lavatory.

"Thirsty Boychy," said Mrs. B.

He looked up at the sky, abstractedly.

"Why so distant, sweetest?" she asked.

"Who, me?"

"No-one else."

"I see."

"Last week of silly old hot metal and then nice new televisions for Boychy in Holborn. Boychy with all the clever lawyers and people where he belongs. Daddy was on the phone earlier."

Boychester brightened.

"He wanted to wish you luck for this week."

"Kind indeed. I shall call him later."

"Mummy's message is she hopes the last pagger's a gagger."

"I'm sure it will be."

"She also said not to worry about the praggers and the metal bagger."

"I shan't, I promise you."

"Oh yes, and a Charles Ffitch with two effs rang and said he's organised, what was it, a little something for Thursday night in the Italian restaurant near the works. What's it called now . . ."

"Domingo's?"

"That's the one. He said I was to tell you it's on him."

"Most civil."

"He sounded awfully nice, actually. Wanted to know whether I would go along as well. I told him sorry but no, because of George. He insisted I got a sitter but I said it was a bit late and that anyway we had 15 hours debt with the circle. Oh, Boychy, it's all for you and the *Bugle*. All in honour of you. Isn't that exciting!"

"I am flattered."

"Well, you shouldn't be. You deserve every bit of it, and more. I did warn him that you'd be reading the last pages on Thursday evening, but he said it didn't matter as you could come and go when you wanted."

Boychester nodded.

"I felt ever so grand for you, Boychy. He said a whole lot of other names, which I can't remember now, of other people who'd be there; councillors and public relations men and other important things like that. Oh, I wish I could remember them. Stupid Mrs. B. He just rattled them off as if I knew them all personally. He kept on saying: 'Oh yes, plus so-and-so and thingummijig'—whoever they were. Wait a minute. Ron Wheeler and Joan. Is that it? They'll be there."

Boychester took it in with another satisfied nod. He was already feeling flushed with the importance of the occasion. He was seeing himself awaiting the arrival of the first last *Bugle* in Domingo's in three days' time, surrounded by all the purchasers of his goodwill. He could hear the toasts ringing from Ffitch and Pimlott. A messenger would come breathlessly through the door, hand him the paper and stand quietly by like waiters did when Buyers tried the wine. The trophy would be passed among the company and none present would forget the day the last post was blown for the metal beast on Boychester's *Bugle*.

Probably a chorus of "For He's a Jolly Good Fellow," followed by long handshakes with a double clasp, and pledges to keep closely in touch through the Holborn era that now dawned. In return, Boychester's promise of continuing support for all their endeavours would be implicit. Thursday would be a great and memorable night. Perhaps Sturridge could be persuaded to come – by someone else, of course.

His anticipation was broken by the sound of George waking from a bad dream and moaning from a window above the garden. Mrs. Boychester sprang from her chair and a few minutes later was back down with the little man clasped to her front.

"Now then," she said grandly, "as a special treat for Jogger, because it's a special week – time for reading. Not silly old books tonight. Instead . . ." she announced it like an ecstatic compere, ". . . Boychy read Message."

"Do you mean the Message to our Readers?" he asked.

"Yes yes. Boychy read Message to our Readers."

If Mrs. B. had wanted to pick something guaranteed to send the child back to sleep, she couldn't have done better. But her motives were not as subtle as that.

"Very well," said Boychester. "You shall hear it." He took his typescript from inside his jacket and solemnly put on his glasses. "But first I want you to promise me something. Both of you. Are you listening, George?"

"Jogger listening," said Mrs. B.

"And that is," Boychester continued, "that you shall not, on your oath, divulge the contents of this to anyone. Now, is that clear?"

George looked perplexed, and Mrs. B. said "Clear."

"It is subject to an embargo – and you know what that is – until Friday."

George managed a bemused nod.

"Very well then," said Boychester. "Just so long as that is understood. No talking about it at school. No mentioning it to the other children of the district."

George shook his head in something like fear.

Boychester cleared his throat and read: "For well over a century now the *Bugle* has brought you all the news that is fit to print. Yes, and sometimes even a little more. We have boldly trodden the path of objective excellence, neither touching a forelock to the establishment, nor succumbing to sectional pressures. We have, in short, been your paper."

George wondered at the strange change that had come over children's literature and stifled a yawn as his father looked up. He might even have been asking himself the question: "Whither Peter Rabbit?"

Boychester read on: "As the popular song so eloquently stated, The Times They Are A-Changing, and the *Bugle*, ever true to its credo, is changing with them. A change for the better. A change for you."

"Wonderful, Boychy! Wonderful!" said Mrs. B.

"We are proud to tell you that as from next week we shall be combining the best of the new with the finest of the old as our printing techniques switch to those of the new technology. It is a change we must view in triumph and with pride. We hope you will do the same. On page five of today's paper we print a detailed guide to the workings of our revolutionary processes – for your enlightenment. It is an important document testifying to the excellence and ingenuity of our nation's technocracy. We hope you will cut it out and keep it."

George was sleeping now and not even Mrs. B.'s shaking could rouse him.

Boychester read on: "Accuracy will walk hand in hand with efficiency. The lion of integrity will lie down with the lamb of objectivity. We shall never shrink from the onerous task of exposing falsehood and hypocrisy as we find it. In our pages, as in life, the lowly may be exalted and the mighty humbled. The mirror which we hold to the world shall brook no distortions. Place your order now. Available from all leading local newsagents."

Boychester took off his glasses and folded the sheet.

Mrs. B. was applauding around George's slumped shape. He was moving from side to side at each clap.

"Oh, brilliant, Boychy," she cried.

"It's far from bad," he said.

She stood up and carried the child inside. On her way she said: "And court tomorrow. What a week."

"Alas, yes. A man is up on a bizarre yet grave charge. I must be there to see fair play."

"Kind Boychy."

Almost exactly twenty-four hours later Cathal was in the same place – the bar of the Chairmen. The pub was full tonight. Outwardly little had changed. Mick was pouring the bottom half of the poteen bottle for the same three, and Maire was leaning on the bar, breaking away every so often to serve a customer. Thousands Were Sailing to America, sent by Ron Wheeler and Joan. It might have been the previous evening, except that it wasn't.

The main difference was that between that time and this, Cathal had become a convict and indebted to Her

Majesty to the tune of £40. The transports of the nineteenth century never knew such guilt. The day had passed in a blur, and Cathal had no clear recall of any events since the previous evening. The scene from the courtroom came back at him like a dream. He would have wiped it out like Hubbard at the screen if only he could. But the presence of the two PRs, sitting smugly on the bench as they had done that morning at the back of the court, made escape impossible.

Boychester had also been there, very round faced, very orange and mock-glum. Camina, bless him, had sidled in at the back a minute later, unknown to Boychester. The two nuns of course had been there. For the life of him Cathal could not remember whether they had spoken or had had their statements read by another. Anyway, it didn't matter now. The cruel puritanism that such a lovely brogue could conceal was not worth the search.

The queer policeman. He had been there too, looking up with the sympathy which regrettably his people would not let be translated into practical help. His surface had looked even more downcast than Boychester's as the obscene tale had unfolded. He had had his initialled brief-case with him still, and for a few seconds Cathal had found himself concentrating on the parting and the greasy hair last seen from the window of The Trenches.

And who else? Why, Mrs. Weekes naturally. He had never seen a pen so sharp or busy, nor the pages of a notebook turn so quickly. She was always dapper, but today she had been Sunday-smart and looking up eagerly at every exchange. There had also been a girl next to her, a niece, not unlike her in the face, dressed as well for the Townswomen's Guild. Occasionally she would nod as Mrs. Weekes leant over to explain something in a whisper.

Both she and her aunt had reminded Cathal of nothing more than those women he had seen while covering a point-to-point in Sussex years ago. Particularly on the younger one there had been that haughtiness of county stock awaiting a spectacle. In fact Cathal had got her wrong. Her expression had been one of concern – she had felt desperately sorry for this man – and any traces of contempt which he might have picked up had not been for him but for the scribbling aunt.

Had that been the full complement, Cathal wondered again: Boychester, the queer policeman, the sisters, Joan, Ron Wheeler in the bum-freezer, Camina at the back, Mrs. Weekes and the young niece at the front. Then there had been all the clerks running here and there with bits of paper, and the uniformed policemen around the door, smiling sycophantically like butlers towards the bench from time to time.

On the bench itself, two middle-aged men either side of a slightly younger woman. She could have been going out for the evening, Cathal had thought; gloves, earrings, hair expensively stacked up like a cloud. And that voice. What a voice that had been; more like the Queen's than the Queen's own. Cathal had felt sordid and exposed even to be under the same roof as her, never mind the fact that she was there to pore over the legal niceties of his arse. It had been like having a peer inspect him for syphilis in full view of a restaurant. That had definitely been the worst of it; to cross paths with this polished creature from another world. To have her attention, take her time. And his arse of all things as the linking factor. The £40 fine had been pure relief beside that. Oh, those measured tones, full of tolerance and sweet reason. Advice from the left, advice from the right, and that blameless face swaying from one whisper to the other as Cathal's knuckles had turned white on the rail below him. A husband in the city, no doubt, two teenage children, and an ocean of time now at the disposal of rectitude.

Then there had been the general public, men and women of all ages; *tricoteuses* knitting in the shadow of the guillotine. And Cathal's own name on the charge sheet, the sheet to which he had gravitated first thing in a morning of court work for 20 years. It had contained the names of half a dozen other doomed felons, drunks and house-breakers. And now his own name on it. For a while, as he stood exhibited there, he had thought himself at his own inquest, following the drama of his last days and hours as they were unfolded by sobbing friends with the usual painful precision. With the voices passing through him he had fancied he might have heard a pathologist say that the deceased was well nourished, and a cousin declare that the deceased had appeared rather depressed on his last visit.

Except that the Chairman of the Bench had been no coroner, unless she was presiding over an autopsy on the last shreds of Cathal's dignity. The words "£40", spoken crisply, like an auctioneer's last price, had been as welcome as death to a cancer victim.

After that, everything grew even fainter to Cathal in the Chairmen. There had been a general shifting of people as he had stepped down and Mrs. Weekes had flitted back to the start of her notes. The niece had looked sullen. He had also been aware of Boychester making for the magistrate with a broad smile.

During the afternoon he had wandered the streets, he couldn't be sure where, until opening time and Maire at the optic. Quite unaware of the hour, he had gone down old streets suddenly abbreviated by corrugated iron and rising scaffold behind; roads with houses blinded by breeze blocks in the front windows; unknown little parks that skulked behind the terraces; boys with faces dirty from sweets playing on the swings and looking at him as if he were about to ask them some strange question; railings behind which girls were playing netball on a re-marked tennis court. Maybe he had wandered twice past some of these places, looking for familiar street names that would spark a pattern back towards the Chairman.

One thing, however, he could recall from the five hours between court and pub; in an overcast little park, where mothers wheeled their prams among the slides and merry-go-rounds, he had met a familiar face. The eyes had been very vacant and flickering behind the glasses, and the voice seemed to have risen a tone or two from the one Cathal could remember. In spite of this and other changes, there could be no mistaking the man. His hair had been razed short at the back and temples and he had been wearing a square, badly fitting jacket of thin blue cotton. His gait had been like a blind man's shuffle, one leg feeling its way forward tentatively in front of the other. Deep in their own shock, the two men had come face to face with each other near a bench. Cathal had wanted to say "Sizer" and shake him by the hand, but the other's institutionalised look had given out awful fragility.

"The Irishman from the *Bugle*," Sizer had said. "Yes, yes. From the *Bugle*."

"Well that's correct," Cathal had answered, surprised at being remembered.

"And how does it all go? Well, well. The Irishman from the *Bugle*. I have a senior position with a major marketing concern. Major marketing concern. On the administrative side, I am. Yes, something I always wanted to try my hand at. Ha ha. Good Heavens. Fancy that. Nice car I have. Automatic. Headrests."

Hinging straight from the waist, he had said in a loud but confidential voice: "Expense account. Well out of Hubbard's place . . . still, thrusting along, are you, I expect, Mr. Dwyer? Good, good, jolly good. All the new stuff in, I read. Going over to newtech. Just the job, just the job. About time, of course. The only way. No alternative. Well, well, fancy seeing you. Got to go. Meeting an account. Big one. Ha ha."

Cathal had been about to make some remark like "I'm sorry, old chap. Really, so sorry," but Sizer had passed on with a stiff wave towards the park gate and his dismal room in the block nearby owned by the after-care fellowship to which he had been referred from Epsom.

An hour or so later Cathal had finally found his way to the Chairmen.

"Don't take on, Cathal," Mick was saying. "You mustn't take on so. We'll drink to a bad blow on the *Bugle* for Boychester."

"Well, I'm in it," said Cathal.

"So if that's how it's to be, that's how it's to be."

"In the *Bugle* and in the shit."

"Well it's a rag anyway. Except when you write in it."

"I am written in it."

"It doesn't deserve you, Cathal."

The pub had filled up now and the two sides of Kerry beef were standing in the corner. They recognised Cathal and guessed from his state that they could expect another performance.

They were to be disappointed. When they looked up from their mugs again they saw Cathal by the bar leaning forward as rigid as a bowsprit, at 45 degrees. His eyes were two red globes staring in unutterable outrage at some spot miles away. Suddenly the wind dropped, and like Crowley before him he was lying broken at the foot of the cliff.

VI
The Final Issue

THE FOLLOWING MORNING, Wednesday, Boychester was earlier than usual for work. There were only a few other vehicles, belonging to the printers, in the car park. He got out and walked in through the silent press room where tomorrow night the cylinders would be whirring his *Bugle* – Reader's Message, Cathal Dwyer's court case and all – through to the packer's belt of spindles. A man in overalls was kneeling down with an oil gun at the base of the machinery. Boychester passed by, and climbed the metal stairs. Up in the linotype area just two men were clicking their keyboards, and for once the noise failed to blot out the sound of a tinny radio turned up to a distorting volume. Further along the works, on the stone, an old man waiting for the late trays of metal was sipping tea and filling in a pools coupon. Across the empty floor the West Indian carding the lead was surrounded by a group of the suited men who were ignoring him and pointing with pencils around the tops of the walls.

In the newsroom Mrs. Weekes sat alone, enthralled by the new Irish Pinkie which she was holding between her fingers. She was looking as smart as on the previous day, with a chiffon neck scarf knotted under her chin. She was reading aloud: "Mr. Dwyer told the bench he could not remember the events of the morning in question."

She looked up as the editor entered, and beamed: "Good morning, Mr. Boychester!"

"And to you, indeed, Mrs. Weekes," he replied. "And to you. Charming niece well, I trust?"

"Yes, very. But right off the idea of newspapers, I'm afraid."

"Because of yesterday."

"Mmm."

"It's a hard business we're in, Mrs. Weekes. There is little place for emotion."

"So I told her. Young Zoe's a bit of a bleeding heart, you know."

"We are professionals, Mrs. Weekes. No fears and no favours. Remember: the public's right to information. Free access at all times."

"My views entirely."

"The world has warts. We are not cosmeticians, nor should we be."

He was pleased with the last line and passed through into his office to add it in biro to the Message. Neither yesterday afternoon, while Cathal was wandering the streets, nor this morning did he comment on the Irishman's absence, although it was his clear right to do so. Compassion, guilt, or indifference: it could have been any of these feelings that kept him silent. But the last one was the only safe bet.

At his desk he opened the proofs of the special inside spread on new technology. Diagrams like those projected on to the screen in the boardroom at Holborn several months ago littered the two pages. He scanned the column upon column of text extolling the virtues of the new way, and scribbled some amendments in the margin. It was an impenetrable spread, the fruit of a collaboration between Boychester and Sturridge, in which the ex-Compucomp man had had it all his own way. A reader would need a degree in electronics and a morning to spare if he was to get anything out of it. Sturridge had assumed that the readers would have both and had slapped down Boychester's suggestion that microcircuitry might be a rather specialised field. The only part of the spread which bore the editor's hand was the large headline which ran all the way across the top: "Your at-a-glance guide to the New Technology," with the smaller words underneath: "A plain man's view of the latest in newspaper production." Sturridge had jibbed even at this, complaining that it made it look as if he himself was a plain man, which he wasn't. One criticism he didn't raise was that the guide was not easy to follow and so the headline was misleading.

The phone rang and Boychester answered; it was Charles Ffitch: "Charles, hi. Yah, wife told me. Incredibly civil. No, really, can't thank you enough. . . . What do you mean, last minute? No, it's absolutely fine. I'm delighted. . . . Well, she'd have told you on the dog and bone; no can do. Right, because of the kids. You'll know one day . . . oh come on now Charles, course you WILL. Anyway, yes, I wouldn't not accept for the world. Shade embarrassing, mind – all those chaps and chappesses you've jacked up. Eh? No, I'm not fishing. Oh, if you must. Fire away . . . Really? The mayor, no less. Pulling my leg. OK, so a promise is a promise, but frankly I'll believe it when I see it, Chas. Look, this must be setting your people back the odd yen. Yes, I know it's Company. Mr. Sturridge will be incredibly flattered. That's right: Sturridge with a D-G-E. Have you never? Oh, he's a really decent fellow. His number? Sure, right here. Who did you say? Oh, the lady reporter. You mean Mrs. Weekes. Well, as a matter of fact she's right here. If you hang on a tick I'll ask her . . ."

Boychester put the receiver on his desk and went through into the newsroom. Neither he nor Mrs. Weekes had noticed that while he had been speaking to Charles Ffitch and while she had been reading to the bottom of the sixth sheet, Camina had slipped in through the door and was sitting at his desk. He looked worse than ever. His face was a terrible grey colour and there were deeply gouged crescents of black under his glasses, which some take 40 years to acquire.

"Oh, Mrs. Weekes," Boychester said breezily. "Tomorrow night. Domingo's. For a sort of last metal paper do. Charles Ffitch from CKC says can you come."

She preened mightily and made as if to say "Well . . ." As she did so her right leg swung coquettishly over the left knee. He also fancied he saw the kind of twinkle in her eye as the one he had got from Bobsy Marshall, and which he kept seeing in middle-aged women ever since breaking his duck of extra-marital affairs.

"That's settled then," he pre-empted her. "I'll tell him you'll be there." He went back into his room and continued: "Yah, Charles. That's grand. Says she'd love to. . . . No, that's about the lot from here. Who? The Irishman? Oh Lord alive no. Well, he'll be there, how shall we say, in the letter if not in the spirit."

He let out a huge guffaw which kept going until he had squeezed his lungs empty. Ffitch didn't get the joke, but he laughed dutifully, one of his reception-laughs.

By the time Boychester had finished his conversation, Pam and Harvey had appeared, he two minutes after her, still trying to keep up the pretence that they didn't come from the same flat in the morning these days. They exchanged formal good mornings, which wouldn't have fooled Mrs. Weekes, nor even Camina if he had been aware of them. His sleepless eyes were blinking at a spot of desk in front of him. When he became aware of Boychester entering the room he braced himself for an attack of some sort. It didn't come. Boychester acted as though the Jew wasn't there. No questions about what he was working on, no oblique remarks about Cathal's absence for two days. It was as if the two of them had been expunged, just one more Irishman and one more Jew made stateless – "Not known here" – like many another ghost in The Trenches.

Even in his exhaustion Camina could sense the strengthening alliance between Boychester and Mrs. Weekes. The two of them were inspecting the pink sheets which were carrying Cathal's blush towards posterity. Boychester was murmuring: "Very good, very good," and Mrs. Weekes was preening again.

Not even Pam or Harvey appeared to be acknowledging Camina. From his jacket he took the envelope which had dropped on to the hall floor of The Trenches that morning. He opened it. After the normal gambit in which his mother offered food and laundry and a bed for the weekend "whenever you are round these parts", as though he were with Bobsy Marshall's husband in Guinea-Bissau, she went on to speak warmly of the new au pair. She had a little brother who was crazy about board games, although if David wanted to pick them up he could do so at any time. Also, his room was still there for him if he needed it "more permanently". He had only to write – as if phoning would amount to an admission that he had only been three miles away all the time.

After some more small talk about the rabbi's gout and

the kidney failure of the neighbour's dog – such things were always the lull before the storm – she wrote that they were both very distraught at the news of Sacha's death. He had come back from a business trip to Israel, "looking marvellous," but had then got terrible pains. The doctors had opened him up to find him riddled with cancer. "Fortunately it didn't take long," she wrote. "Of course he was cheerful to the last, but obviously a little on the thin side as you would expect. Your father is very upset and has had bilious attacks. Pavlovsky and the rest have rallied round wonderfully and have spent much time here. I have told your father he must cut down on work, but he doesn't listen to me. Another of his friends from the old days – you remember Lorenz Green – had a thrombosis in his leg and was told not to fly. He ignored them, and he died also, at Gatwick. David, if you could only have a word with him, I am sure he would take notice.

From your loving mother.

Camina folded the letter. The trouble and anxiety hanging in that well-carpeted house in Hampstead washed over him completely. He could feel nothing for it. He thought of that eternal smell of pile in the hall, and of the little harp-like device on the back of the door that jangled when someone came in. But there was something affronting about being drawn back into the grief of that *ménage*. As an attempt to reclaim him from whatever troubles his life had brought him in this foreign part of the city, it was fruitless. Camina was blind and deaf to such pleas. Last night's dream was with him still: the sergeant on the duckboards again, looking on in satisfaction with the two civilians as the corpse of the corporal was swung into the mud; and he, Rosenberg, wanting to scream aloud just before waking, but with his voice plucked out by a huge clanking bird that had darkened the sky and snapped its beak deep into his larynx. What hurt him now, and would have done so even more acutely if he had had the mental energy to spare, was the fact that only misery of the Hampstead kind was expected to touch him.

All morning and most of the afternoon he sat like this in the newsroom. Boychester came and went, Mrs. Weekes prattled inanely on the phone, first to Zoe, then, he thought, to the clerk of the court, and then to Zoe again. Not once that he was aware of did she even glance half his way. Occasionally he could hear Boychester laughing uproariously from his office, that same explosion of false mirth, tailing off for as long as he could hold it, just like his signature. Printers also came in and out, holding proofs between their hands like tablecloths and cussing under their breath as Mrs. Weekes told them that the great man was still on the phone.

Pam and Harvey were muted in their intimacy and, like the rest, ignored Camina. He felt invisible, spectre-thin. People would look over his head at the calendar on the wall, or up to his right where a list of phone numbers was pinned. They would pass behind him, shaking the back of his chair with a hip. But never a word in his direction, nor a puzzled look at Cathal's still empty place.

One of the trees outside in the memorial garden rustled and blew, and at every larger gust its branches would click against the dusty window. By four o'clock the sky was lowering like a winter evening. Dark clouds were passing above the building and the first drops of a shower fell as long as bicycle spokes against the panes. Camina's head ached and he could feel a tacky taste rise into his back teeth and gum his tongue against his palate. Still Boychester's triumphant laugh rang out from the far end, and still Mrs. Weekes made calls.

At about five o'clock he stood up and left. No questions asked. In the works some more metal had arrived and there was a flurry of activity on the stone. A cheerful old printer with white hairs sprouting above his shirt said "Evening, son," but Camina didn't answer. The linotype area was completely empty and downstairs in the press room the man with the oil gun was fixing a new pin-up to the wall.

Through the car-park and past an articulated paper lorry where two men with crowbars were perched on top of the giant rolls, Camina found himself in Fountain Street. He scratched his head and felt in his trouser pocket for enough money to take a taxi. It wasn't there and he set off briskly past the closed door of the Chairmen, and northwards. The rain had stopped and the air was still warm and close with moisture. Towards Brondesbury, where Camina took the broad and quiet back streets there hung a nutty smell of leaves washed down from the trees by the first gusting of autumn. It was a clean smell and a mellow one, but to Camina it reeked of sadness and of walking home alone from school as the late afternoons drew in and the street lamps went on early enough to darken the rest of the day prematurely and throw circles of light into the drizzle on the pavements.

He walked under a metal railway bridge which was echoing with the wheels on the track above. One of the three-coach trains was pulling out of the station. For Camina this whole area was redolent of Boychester; the little line which was championed with such smug patronage, the double-fronted houses and tree-lined roads to which he was always referring, and round the corner the burgeoning shape of Larch Towers. Camina had passed this way with Cathal late one night some months ago just to view the Boychestral home in a sort of inverted sentimental journey. On that occasion the peacock inside had been showing his feathers very co-operatively. The drawing room curtains had been open and Boychester had been going round the table with a decanter. Three men often seen by Cathal from the press gallery of the council chamber had been sitting there, smoking and laughing. The spiritual headquarters of the community had been kindly left open for the scrutiny of the passer-by.

This afternoon Mrs. B.'s huge red head was looking out from the same window. At her waist was George. In the half-light on the pavement she thought she recognised the Jewish profile that passed above the hedge, but she couldn't place it. Camina felt a stab of disgust at seeing the clean bosom of the Boychester family, and remembered Cathal's remark about the mating habits of toads – the little male like a limpet on the back of the larger female – in relation to the couple.

The once-small school across the road had two lights burning in the top floor. From one of the windows a cleaner with a scarf tied round her neck and a cigarette in her mouth that was making her grimace shook a duster into the air.

Coming down the pavement towards Camina was the dumpy figure of Bobsy Marshall, who in the last few days had also spent much time observing the front of Boychester Towers. She was looking for signs of her new lover, whose wife didn't understand him either. Since blooming, Bobsy had gone into trousers – elastic slacks of perhaps five years ago, with skiers' loops under the feet. She would pass this way dozens of times every day, always with a batch of envelopes (unstamped) to legitimise the journey. She and Camina thought they recognised each other, but were too absorbed in their own missions to attempt a greeting. Camina glanced back at her as she slowed nonchalantly and injected a wiggle into her walk. From behind, her middle rotated one way then the other, like a tub in an old washing machine.

Camina walked on as the light faded. He picked his way across main roads stiff with cars, ignoring the red figures on the pedestrian lights. Later he crossed the little park where Cathal had met Sizer. As he reached the other side an attendant was sweeping leaves and preparing to lock up. He walked for over an hour, until he was aware of being in a spot higher than the surrounding suburbs. To the south he could see the lights of a main road threading its way out westwards. A plane hung almost motionless in the dark sky, lights blinking on its belly, and away over to the east of the city two more were stacked up in the queue. In the road to his right the rows of houses stopped abruptly and gave way to the flat outbuildings of St. Teresa's. Towering behind the main block of red brick was the hospital's tall new chimney, from which wisps of smoke rose into the evening. The front drive was a crescent of tarmac with large signs at either end, reading "In" and "Out".

Already under the Victorian frieze with its muscular optimism so ironic for such a place, Camina caught the first whiff of surgical spirit and hygiene. It was all the stronger for having to fight the stenches of an old building. Inside the doors, in the bare foyer where two Indian women sat behind the reception desk, a corridor gave off in both directions. Camina fumbled in his pocket for the piece of paper on which he had written "Curie Ward, East Wing." It seemed terrible to him that Cathal should be receiving now in a place that smacked of such impersonal mercy. He followed the signs to the right along the passage, which after 50 yards split three ways. Curie Ward was to the left. Several paces behind a trolley that was coming from the double doors was a young woman breathing deeply, at the very edge of her composure. A second later she seemed to stumble slightly and then burst into tears on the lapel of the man walking next to her.

Through the doors Camina met the Sister's inquiring gaze.

"Mr. C. Dwyer," he said.

"Ah yes. Admitted last night."

Her voice was as Irish as Cathal's – softer of course – but her looks were as dark and Jewish as his own. It was a combination which Camina found very moving. She was about 30, with the same beauty as some of the slighter women in the photos of Rosenberg at the Slade. It seemed natural to Camina that she should speak to him as from a picture; it was consistent with the illusion in which he was surely standing now.

"How is he?" Camina heard himself ask.

"He's poorly, I'm afraid. You may see him, but you must take it easy. It is just you, is it?"

"Just me."

"He is lucid for some of the time. It was not the worst haemorrhage we've had here, goodness no, but the artery is still in spasm."

"What will happen to him?"

"I believe they are planning not to operate."

"Is that a good thing? A good sign?"

"It means they think it would be better if it is allowed to heal itself."

"Is there a good chance it will?"

"We can never be sure with something like this."

"Why no operation?"

"It could be more dangerous to him."

"Is he in danger then? He is in danger." Camina's voice had become pushing, bullying.

"He is not well," said the Sister calmly.

"How did this thing happen? What was the cause?"

"There was a weakness. We all have a weakness somewhere. In his case it is known as an aneurism. A weakness in the wall of an artery in the brain. Many people have such things. With some it never shows. And with others . . . we cannot tell the reason. Would you like to see him now? He is over in the far corner, on the left."

Camina nodded and walked stiffly through into the ward. In the dimness he caught sight of a pale head on the pillow of a bed against the wall immediately to the right. Around the crown the pallor was greyed by the first three days of growth after the shaving. On one side was a livid scar long enough to unseam the whole head like a tin can.

Further along on the same side were two beds screened off by curtains on a high rail. From one of them an elderly couple were leaving glumly, through the parting between the folds. In the opposite corner, at the end of the row, Camina could see the long bony fingers twitching over the high side. He sat down on the chair beside the bed and gently pulled it forward a few inches until he was looking down at the side of the Irishman's face. Cathal's head was on one side, pointing the other way from his outstretched arm. The right knee was raised at a right-angle under the cover. Camina looked at him for fully a minute. The hair was black and strong, but the shoulders and the top of the chest which protruded from the sheets looked wasted and angular – not at all like Cathal standing Colossus-style in his tweed jacket. Without any covering the forearm and wrist too were skinny and hairless.

After another minute he spoke, as if picking up a dropped thread in his conversation. The voice was very weak: "Told the beak where to get off . . . told her good. Told her I had no time for her kind. Told her good."

He drew a slow deep breath and his head swivelled to the right until the nose was pointing straight at the ceiling. Still the eyes were closed. Then he started again: "Beak and bleeding Boychester are like that . . . like that I'm telling you." He pulled the hand off the side and made to lock the fingers into the left one. The right arm swayed above the chest for a second and then fell. "I have a monkey arm. . . . Camina will take away the monkey arm. You are there, Camina."

"I am, Cathal. Don't tire yourself."

"Tire myself be fucked. Seen you when you sat down. Through an eye, and you can't see me through it."

"No, Cathal."

"I have been explaining to them that you will take away the monkey arm." He fumbled with his right arm again to raise the limp one on the other side. "You see, I think one side doesn't work properly. What is your view on the subject?"

"I – I don't know, Cathal."

"They think I am a monkey, only deafer. Well, I heard all the talk about – about aphasia is it, which means to say your old friend is a bit on the fucked side. Your views on the subject, please."

Cathal's head moved through the next few degrees to face Camina directly. Both eyes opened – the left one only dimly – but the right one pierced as it had always done, and Camina had to look away.

"I was observing that one side is busted. Young David, there will be no more cathedralling, for a while. I am sitting it out and lying low for a little . . . like we do when the Black and Tans pass along. No more Colossusing or Cathedralling. Just for a spell."

There was another silence, broken by Cathal mumbling words that Camina couldn't understand. He seemed to be explaining something in a strange language to an absent friend.

He spoke again: "The Partition. The Partition. Now then, no chancers if you please. The Abbey or nothing. Boychester has some of it, with much of Flaherty, which can easily be sprung with two pounds of explosive up the sow-suit arse. You will do that. Also, there is Mr. Parnell. Not a bad fellow at all, but it is bread and water for him until I return. You will note they have given me a drip, which Maire would frown at. She will see me right on that."

There was a moan from the screened bed opposite, and a cry of "Nurse!" The sister walked in briskly.

"There's a grand lass," said Cathal with his crooked new smile. "You Jews do well in Ireland, and we Irish do well in America. Possibly a lecture tour after the Partition. I am considering offers, Camina."

For the next five or ten minutes Cathal was muttering again and drawing long laboured breaths. During this time Camina could pick out a few words, mostly names: Flaherty, Crowley, Mick, Maire, Mr. Parnell, then Crowley once more.

Eventually the Sister was hovering at the end of the bed with a look that said "Last Orders" in the discreetest way.

"It's not so good among the new Sizer's maggots,

Camina. It's so very dark down here. And pretty cold at nights when the current's off. It's no place for a fellow, and that's certain. Make them call me up, lad. This is a bleeding cave. Oh, make them call me up. Liver's running up the white flag. I heard them talking this afternoon, with their clipboards. They must think I'm deaf. Make them call me up."

Camina felt the light pressure of the Sister's hand on his shoulder, and stood up. He was the last visitor in the ward. As he walked towards the double doors he heard the heels of his shoes clicking louder in the emptiness. He turned briefly to see his friend's fingers still fluttering on the side of the bed, and passed through, leaving Cathal to the last two hours of his life.

Outside on the tarmac crescent he walked about ten steps in the fresh air before stopping and wailing deeply into his hands.

In his little office Boychester was putting the final touches to the front page layout. Immediately below the masthead the Message to our Readers basked in its prominence. It was to be set in large bold type and would span four columns. Immediately to the right, bearing out the commitment to no fears or favours, would run the headline: "Flashing Irishman Fined £40." Boychester ran the galley proofs of Mrs. Weekes's report through his fingers, and read to himself: "An Irish journalist was this week fined £40 for what was described by a magistrate as a most insulting episode."

"The court heard that Mr. Cathal Dwyer, 60, exposed himself to two nuns, and that he used foul language to them."

It went on with full details of the hearing for about 1500 words, certainly enough to carry the story in two unbroken strips of type nearly to the bottom of the page. For once the Boychester rule that evidence should not be duplicated was waived in the interests of exhaustiveness. The other unusual feature of the story was the line: "By Barbara Weekes," the largest by-line ever seen in the paper.

In the right-angle formed by this report and the Message was to be a large photo of Messrs Hubbard and Sizer, pictured in Holborn with the new machinery that would in future be producing the *Bugle*. Finding themselves dishonourable graves beneath the legs of the Colossus would be the lesser felons of the week, all brought like Cathal to the check-out counter of the law's supermarket and rung up by Mrs. Weekes at the till: an old widower stealing two pork pies, a pregnant Pakistani shoplifting a bra – no fears and no favours.

Everything was in order. By this time of the week all the inside pages were already set and moulded, leaving just the front to be made up and checked the following evening, Thursday, before the start of the print run.

Just like the drawing room at Boychester Towers on important occasions, the little office was open to the evening, and anyone passing along the front railings of the memorial garden could look up and see the guardian at work. He set his pencils and ruler on one side of the desk, read once again the list of people whom Charles Ffitch had said would be at Domingo's, then clicked off the light by the cord hanging from the ceiling.

The familiar shapes of the newsroom were silhouetted against the window. He walked through the works and felt the beginnings of nostalgia at the sight of all the dormant organs of the metal beast. It was a feeling just strong enough to bring on a mood of forgiveness for whatever inaccuracies the thing had committed in the past. Besides, its days were numbered, while Boychester's best was yet to come.

Back at The Trenches Camina pulled himself wearily up the front steps. Again he had walked back from the hospital, retracing his steps past Boychester Towers, where Bobsy Marshall had still been strolling with her bundle of envelopes, many hours after the last post.

The whole walk had taken him two hours. He had not slept or eaten for two days and a night. He opened the front door and walked past the ghosts on the table. Not known here, any of them. The phrase made Camina wince. Would one of the other occupants of the block slide out of his room some morning soon and mark the same words on C. Dwyer's mail, such as it was, or even on his own? He slouched up the stairs and across the bubbly lino. At about the same time as he turned the key in Cathal's lock a young nurse fresh on her rounds at St. Teresa's was walking urgently from the Irishman's bed to the far end of the ward; she was calling: "Sister, Sister!"

Clothes and newspapers were strewn around the little room, and the unmade bed still bore the imprint of Cathal's body. The pillow too was cleft in the middle, from where he had raised his head for the last time a few hours before the hearing the previous morning. There was a stale smell of tobacco and a nest of cigarette stubs in an ashtray beside the bed. The walls were tinged with orange from the street lamp outside the window. On the pavement below, the same couple were passing as they had done on the night of the maggots. They were a more confident pair now, arms round each other's waist, she giggling and pointing up the path.

A few feet away from Camina was Mr. Parnell's cage on its table. The wheel was silent, but the straw was churned and tossed, like the scene of a recent struggle. The sprung flap on the front seemed to be out of alignment with the rest of the bars. As Camina looked more closely he saw that Cathal must have forgotten to fasten the clasp. A drab patch of white took his eyes down to the floor immediately below. A cat must have got in somehow and defaecated in some scraps of newspaper. But when Camina bent down he saw that the grey shape was in fact the body of Mr. Parnell, bunched up foetally and as dead as Crowley, with his eyes closed and his paws at prayer.

Camina knelt over the little corpse, looking down on a turned head as he had been doing a couple of hours earlier. From the handwriting on the paper among which the hamster was lying he could recognise the Partition. He scooped up the body in the paper between his two hands and placed the lot on the bed, he didn't know why. He would deal with it in the morning. Perhaps he would bury it in the front garden. Perhaps he would burn it. The natural adviser was beyond asking.

Upstairs in his own room Camina undressed wearily and was asleep in the old dream a moment after his head touched the pillow. But it was different tonight. The sergeant on the bridge was alone. The two civilians had gone. Behind Rosenberg two more young men had appeared. They looked like Weinstein and Rotger and were inciting him to violence. Before he could weigh up the consequences of his actions he had advanced towards the sergeant, who looked frightened and was feeling behind him for the railing. The Jew was shaking him by the lapels and striking his fat jaw from side to side, first with the palm and then with the knuckles. The sergeant's neck was being stretched back over the railing near the bright new machine until the gristle of his throat stood out. He was letting out a strangled cry and was promising remission. The Jew felt a madness of power in his arms and carried on with the blows. Another to the right, another to the left, until the first drops of blood came from the knuckles and was splattered with the next strike. He was hoisting the sergeant up by the buttocks on to the top rail, aware of the corpulence and dead weight of the man, and of his own juddering muscles. A moment later the sergeant was letting out a terrible yell and disappearing backwards down towards the mud, with the soles of his feet facing back up at his attacker.

When the Jew looked round his view of Weinstein and Rotger was obscured by a very large woman with a kind face and red hair, and a child at her side. She was screaming. Camina woke here, but tonight in his tiredness he stayed awake for not very long. For the first time he was glad to slide back down into that underworld of dark events instead of struggling with his last breath for a wakefulness that only left him drained in the hours of daylight. But as he slid down now it was to a plain deeper even than the ruined fields and smashed drainage under the mud, where for eight hours he was to lie immune from any intrusion. In his descent he didn't even have time to resent the irony of the best things coming in the smallest parcels.

"Charles, hi."

"Dear Chap!"

"Super."

"Super."

"Golly, quel spread."

"Nonsense, mere nothing. Come through."

"It's packed."

"Just a few friends."

"A few!"

"Drink. G and T?"

"Stiff one, Charles. Bless you. Vieux chapeau, you've done me proud."

Charles Ffitch guided the guest of honour through into the party suite at the back of the restaurant. Domingo himself was there, bowing out of the way obsequiously as Boychester advanced with Ffitch. There was a pricey array of canapés wherever the eye wandered – little coloured pictures under a glaze of aspic – being plucked away from the plates on all sides like breadcrumbs in beaks. There must have been all of forty people packed into the suite, every one of them Boychester's trading partners in the importance business.

Pimlott had collared a member of the finance committee and was leaning with one arm against the wall and flattening the little councillor against it. The crooked face was lunging backwards and forwards, with another confidence at every throw, until the tiny man was screwing up his eyes and standing as stiff as an ironing board for the next attack.

Joan was actually holding Frank Wheeler's hand now, but their straight arms only met at the end, behind her dress and his suede jacket. Every few minutes Domingo would pass round and insist on taking the jacket from him, but each time Frank motioned him away. Some ill will was finding its way into these exchanges.

Joan herself wore a proprietorial look. Not towards Frank, but towards the various officials and elected representatives who, tongues loosened, were peppered round the crowded room. The look was smug, but tinged with apprehension in case these people whose words and deeds it was her chore to launder for public consumption, might take it into their heads to by-pass her. The conditions were dangerously ripe for a breach of that golden rule which was her raison d'être: that contact with the press was maintained only across the bridge which she held. It was all very threatening to her monopoly of the municipal truth. Her eyes darted round the room and returned a message of some comfort. Of the press there was only Mrs. Weekes and now Boychester himself present. Not too much damage could be done. Pimlott was passing a folded slip of paper to his prisoner. He stood back as the little member raised his eyebrows dutifully at the figure written there.

Mrs. Weekes was advancing towards Boychester at the mouth of the suite when a dumpy figure jostled into her shoulder from the left. It was Bobsy Marshall in a terrible trouser suit, with stitches that lived in danger of being wrenched apart at the thighs. The two women reached the hero in a dead heat and hugged him simultaneously on each side. A kiss smacked out on either cheek and their hands closed round the other one's arms and shoulders on opposite sides of his neck. For several seconds the knot of hands grappled and Boychester was lost. When he reappeared he saw Sturridge across the room. He was being quizzed on new technology by an eager young lady from the Labour benches. He had deflected her well and she was casting about for an alternative to this walking seminar.

Was that the chairman of the magistrates' bench over there? Yes, it was, and surely that was her husband with her. Boychester almost swam through the throng towards them. While she talked she put out one hand to touch the approaching editor's sleeve – a sort of engaged tone – before saying: "So brave."

"Ma'am?"

"So very brave of you."

"I am unworthy of this."

"I know of few other editors who would have done it. To say fairly and squarely before the whole community – a vigilant one, no small thanks to you – 'We shall not bow to that censorship which is to our own advantage.'"

"Ma'am, I have no choice."

"Oh, but that's just it. It speaks through your every pore that you are a man of compassion. No, don't look embarrassed, I'm not tiddly. Through your every pore. And of course you would have done everything reasonably in your power not to cause undue hardship to that Irishman. Dowd was it?"

"Dwyer."

"That's right. You would have spared your brother Dwyer if it had been humanly, or perhaps I should say humanely, possible. And so you did have a choice. Why, there are any number of precedents for the fellows of a profession closing ranks against the law. Mr. Boychester, we even do it ourselves. No no, you had a choice and you made the bold, painful decision. To publish and be damned. No fears and no favours. You put the Press on trial and it was found not guilty. May God go with you to Holborn."

"My profoundest thanks to you, ma'am."

"No. Mine to you. It was a breath of fresh air. My husband, Gerald here, says he has an analogy. Gerald."

"It was," said the wealthy man plummily, "it was like a father giving his son out LBW at the parents' cricket match."

"But not quite, Gerald dear. The Irishman was considerably older."

"Well then, like a son giving his father out LBW."

"Except," said the JP. "that that would entertain the possibility of mischief, which was here absent."

Gerald tried again: "Of course, much would have depended upon the straightness of the ball."

"I think not, dear," said his wife as the mayor's paunch barged into the little group. He was a huge, ruddy butcher, medium rare all over, a contentious choice by the majority group. He now had a chain of shops, a chain of office, and a history of suspected graft to which Boychester's ear was deaf, never more than now. The mayor was drunk and very loud:

"Wonderful what they're doing, innit? Bleeding marvellous. Just been down St. Lukes with the wife. Fabulous little do. All the poor little kiddies with spina whatsit. Didn't see your photographer chappie there. Still, never mind. Bloody wonderful though. You know, something to live for. Nurses younger than my own daughter. Just little girls, bless their cotton socks, but bloody angels just the same. Wanted to cry. Best year of my life, this. Then up to the Cumnor Centre for the old folks. Smashing little do. Old man Cumnor would've loved it all, bless him. And then on to here. Where are we anyway? No, no, only joking, only joking. Ha ha. Old and the new, Mr. Boychester, old and the new. That's what I've been doing today. Young ones, ancient ones. Weenies and grannies. And blow me down, that's what we're doing now, innit? Out with the old, in with the new, eh? Well then, there you are. Blooming marvellous, I say. The whole thing. I'm pissed, but don't tell Joan. She'll be after me with a chloroform napkin. Ha ha. Got to circulate. Bloody marvellous though. Just the ticket. Must go and check Harris is still on orange juice. Don't want another shunt in Scrubs Lane. Last one cost the ratepayers a few p. Only got to piss on the headlamp and you need a new wing. Can't get off for under a grand. Has to go up to Stevenage or something. I don't know. Joan'll know. Buggered if I'm going to sod about in some jumped-up Austin for a week. They all want a Roller don't they. Course they do and can't blame them. Don't we all. Ha ha. Bet Harris is pissed. Going to sniff his Britvic. Ha ha. Bloody marvellous though. Love all this."

Heads broke away from their conversations as Boychester passed among them.

"Dear boy," said Ffitch.

"You're a gentleman," said Joan.

"The very best," said Frank Wheeler.

"Only the threshold," said Sturridge.

"Apparently J. D. wanted 50 K.," said Pimlott.

"So brave," said the J. P.

"LBW," said her husband.

"I've been proud," said Mrs. Weekes.

"What a man," said Bobsy Marshall.

"Best year of my life," said the mayor.

"Must sober up," said Harris.

"More drink for Signor Boychester," said Domingo.

As the landscape of admiration swam before and around him, Boychester remembered the front page proof still lying in his office. He couldn't tell quite how long he had been in Domingo's. An hour? An hour and a half? Maybe more. Soon the head printer would be coming into the newsroom, asking for it. Oh well, it was all read and checked, with all the amendments in the margin. That was good enough. The printer would have to pick it up for himself this time, instead of having it delivered on to the stone. It would do no harm. Besides, tonight was a bit special. There was nothing to worry about. Boychester was set for the evening. Why should he return? It was raining now. The walk would take ten minutes or more. Even above the Musak that Domingo had put on ("Wops groaning with pasta," said the mayor), the drops on the flat roof could be heard. A guest of honour had his duties. He would not shirk them. He drank again. His admirers swirled into a single benevolent smile. Now he was dancing with the J. P. and a space had cleared in the middle of the floor. "Howzat!" said the husband. Now he was dancing with Mrs. Weekes. Now Bobsy Marshall was wrenching him from her, publicly. Next was Joan, with one arm stiffly round his waist and the other palm flat on his shoulder. More couples joined them: Pimlott and the Labour member, Ffitch and Bobsy Marshall, Frank Wheeler and Mrs. Weekes, the mayor and a waitress, Harris by himself, smooching into the air.

The music grew louder and the time passed.

The profile looked particularly Jewish and haggard against the plate window at the front of the restaurant. He loitered there for a moment, with his coat collar pulled hard across his jaw in case someone who knew him should come out at that moment. It could be Joan, Frank Wheeler, any one of them. Above the throb of the music he could hear the party – the whoops from the waitress being driven back by the mayor's paunch, Bobsy's yell of delight at catching Boychester again, Pimlott's roar of disbelief at something the little councillor had said.

Camina had walked from Fountain Street. Standing by the railing of the memorial garden he had looked up at the lit window of Boychester's office and the dimmer glow from the newsroom next to it. He had stayed there for several minutes, and seeing no shadows moving on the ceiling, no silhouette through the glass, he had taken his vigil to Domingo's.

Now he started away from the restaurant again as the party noise exploded from the door and the mayor burst on to the pavement, puffing hard from the efforts of cradling the waitress above his paunch. He was setting her down on the pavement and demanding to drink champagne from her shoe. She was screaming coquettishly for Domingo and complaining of the rain, while he threatened terrible reprisals.

Camina's guess was right. Boychester was dug in for the evening and would probably not see the front page again until the messenger bore the first copy, as instructed, to the party. There was a risk, of course. At any time Boychester might decide to return and throw his weight about on the stone. That was always possible, some would say probable. If he did, and if Camina now carried out what he was intending, it would be a fair cop, fairer by far than Cathal's.

Camina computed all this as he hurried on down the wet pavement. His walk gave way to a trot. By now the rain had got through his hair and was running in rivulets down his face. It was a drizzle that looked fine and filmy, but it drenched. His trot gave way to a run. Soon his shoes were splashing round the corner into Fountain Street, where the Chairmen was disgorging. The usual men were coming one by one through the doorway, weighing up the drop from the step to the pavement and leaning heavily against the side with one arm. Camina picked his way through them and after a few more paces came level with the railings of the memorial garden. He paused, looked at the rounded points above the bar which joined the railings at the top, about head height, then glanced back down at the little throng outside the pub. He carried on slowly round the whole block, passed the locked car park and loading bay, and the crack of light that came through the double doors next to the rolling rack.

He turned left and left again, along the back of the works. The walls were sheer and almost blind, like a workhouse, with just a few small-paned windows ranged across, a few feet below the guttering. By the time he got round to the Chairmen again the crowd had gone.

Only Mick was standing in the doorway, next to Maire, watching the back of the last customer disappear. Camina paused again until he saw the door close and Mick's shadow stretch up and then down behind the glass to push the bolts home. If he saw Camina he would only press him for news of his favourite customer. Cathal would not have wanted that, tonight of all nights.

Camina was again level with the railings. The street was empty. He tightened his hands around two of the metal points, and then moved his right hand onto the next one for a better pull. He flexed his arms and felt the instep of his right foot against the top bar. He strained the leg straight until a sharp pain stabbed him in the side of the groin. The next thing he felt was the pressure of the little points jabbing the front of his body from the neck to the knees, and then he splayed heavily down into the flower bed like a high jumper.

He picked himself up, brushed the wet earth from his trousers, and hurried across the corner of the lawn until he stood against the wall on the bed directly below Boychester's window. The drainpipe in front of his nose had a convenient inch or two of space between itself and the wall. It was fixed firmly by large metal brackets at intervals of two feet. He pulled up again and struggled for a purchase with his soles against the wet bricks. Only by jamming his toes into the gap behind the pipe until they hurt could he climb. With his whole body juddering, just as it had done in the final dream, he made the two or three upward thrusts he needed to lock one hand round the ledge of the first floor window sill. One last heave and he lifted himself so that most of his weight rested on his palms on the sill. One half of the hinged window was ajar. He pulled it outwards and tried in vain to jackknife his right leg up and plant the foot next to the hands. It was no use. He worked himself forward so that he hung on his stomach across the ledge, legs dangling back into the air, head thrust down into Boychester's office a couple of feet from the proof on the desk. He thought fleetingly of Cathal on the front steps of The Trenches when the nuns passed. If the printer came in now he was finished. But that was not due to happen for another half-hour.

Once more he pushed forward with his hands on the inside of the wall and then took his full weight on the floor. The Hollywood artefact which Boychester had imagined during his train ride to Weybridge could not have been a more menacing sight to the absentee editor.

Camina's jacket flapped down around his ears. His legs clattered down behind him and he was in. On the desk, next to the proof, was a neat little row of pencils and biros, one of which had made the various markings in the margin and the big arcs that swooped into the midst of the print to locate the errors.

Standing at the desk, with Boychester's own chair touching the backs of his knees, Camina scanned the page: the loathsome Message at the top – "the male toad position," he said to himself – and to the right the even viler report of Cathal's case. ("The guilty shall not elude us through death," he muttered in mock-Boychester.) In the centre of the broadsheet were the grainy faces of Sturridge and Hubbard, with the old man's eyes sharp even through the poor reproduction; below that the petty criminals, lined up at the bottom in order of their unsought statuses. If this one had made another inch, then that one would have been spared. One man's guilt is another man's innocence. How true that seemed to Camina as his eye moved back up and across to Cathal, who even posthumously was putting a heavy subsidy into Boychester's moral uprightness. With its mixture of obsequiousness, sycophancy and sheer plain bullying, the page seemed to Camina the complete expression of its creator's character. But how vulnerable it was now in his absence, spread there like a doped patient. He placed a paperweight on one edge and a heavy ash tray on the other, and thought again of the last dream, with the sergeant's arms pinioned against the bridge rail. "So Boychester," he said aloud, "you would scent your sty with a corpse, would you?" One man's guilt, another man's innocence.

Gingerly he opened the door into the newsroom and stepped back quickly as he saw the nightwatchman's head and shoulders through the glass panel, passing by along the corridor. He was swigging from a small bottle and humming as he shuffled. When he had gone, Camina walked to the far door, past Mrs. Weekes's pile of Pinkies with Cathal and his fellow victims of the week freshly laid on the top. He clicked the door closed before returning to Boychester's office. If the printer came in, or Boychester for that matter, Camina might have just enough time, after hearing the door open, to scramble over the window ledge and drop the ten feet down into the memorial garden. He took up one of the biros and sat down at the desk. Everything was silent. His heart pounded inside his chest. From somewhere beyond Fountain Street came the two tones of a police car horn. The drizzle was still falling. The nib hovered lower and lower over Cathal's case, the wretched obituary. Then Camina set to work feverishly. His first strokes ran a bold squiggle through the headline. Next to it he wrote "delete" and ran another line up into untenanted space high in the right margin. Here he wrote in square, impersonal capitals the words: "Editor fined £40 for Gross Indecency." He then worked his way systematically down the story, substituting the name Boychester at every mention of Dwyer. The age, 60, he left unaltered, so too the by-line of Barbara Weekes. The address he changed simply to Boychester Towers, Brondesbury.

Except for the first few paragraphs the alterations were not gross. In her usual style, designed to claim some spin-off from the dignity of officialdom, Mrs. Weekes had peppered the copy with such phrases as "the accused was said to have . . ." and "it was alleged that the defendant had . . ."

Boychester and his court reporter may not have fancied themselves as cosmeticians, but for Camina the surgery was elementary. The new convict fitted the features perfectly. The story made absolute sense. Strange that it should be here, right here in the inflated posterity of crime that the two men, so different, should be merged and metamorphosed and sent on their new ways, Boychester to his new infamy, Cathal to his second oblivion. Camina's nib and eye accelerated as he worked towards the end, hurriedly wiping the Irishman away from any shared ground with Boychester. One man's guilt.

As he re-read the corrected proof, just one thing bothered Camina. It was in the second paragraph, at the first striking out of Cathal Dwyer. What was Boychester's first name? What the hell was it. This was absurd. It must simply have slipped Camina's mind. Yet how could it? There must surely have been people, here in the building, who used the Christian name. The head printer? Sturridge, when he was about? Mrs. Weekes? No, with them it was always Mr. Boychester. What about the large red-headed wife? Who did she ask to speak to whenever Camina picked up the phone? Boychy. It was always Boychy. Or else The Editor. Camina opened a drawer in the desk for some guidance from an envelope or a list. But the few odd letters he could find gave nothing away. They too just had The Editor, or Mr. Boychester, Editor. So Boychester was merely Boychester. To friends and associates, nothing other than Boychester. This wasn't good enough. Oh, for a birth certificate or the phone number of a Boychester cousin, if such a person existed. Camina remembered that local importance had left the man with no choice but to go ex-directory, so the phone book was no help. "An enforced anonymity." That had been the phrase.

Camina didn't delay any longer. He searched his mind for a name, any name. What was Boychester, in terms of a Christian name? He didn't bother to debate the matter long. He lowered his wrist again and made to write "Claude" in the margin, but at the last minute settled for "Helmut." Then he addressed himself to the rest of the page and the handful of amendments to be made there.

Helmut Boychester, 60, was still just about dancing, but his arms had given up all attempts to hold a partner. The partners, Bobsy Marshall and Mrs. Weekes, were doing all the holding necessary. Whenever the music paused, the other woman – whichever it was – would move forward for her turn. At the moment it was the miserable Bobsy who was sitting it out, biting her nails back to the quick and doing her washing-machine sway, on her own. Boychester's downward thrust was very downward – the chin, the shoulders, the limp little arms, everything. He was speaking an oral leader, full of misprints, to the honoured Mrs. Weekes: "It was, was it not, Mr. Cole Porter, who in another era observed that Anything Goes. Have we come so far since the days of that prophetic utterance? The answer is surely No."

"Splendid, Mr. Boychester!" said Mrs. Weekes. She was trying to plump him up, cushion-like, by the elbows into a proper dancing position, but Domingo's special measures had taken their toll. The face was very orange, and sweating profusely. Twice he had tried to leave, and twice he had failed. At the first attempt Charles Ffitch had yelled for silence, made an appalling speech from a table top and read his own poem, which had ended:

"So now to Holborn's hallowed parts
Our conquering hero bears his arts.
Whom do I speak of? Why, you've guessed, sir.
Freedom's Friend – the Great Boychester!"

On the second attempt he had got as far as the door, only to be hauled back by the mayor, who had bellowed: "Whoa! Hey, everyone. He's trying to get away!" Boychester had been dragged back into the fray to drunken shouts of "Shame!"

Now he launched his third bid. "The proof," he said. "I should see the proof." His speech had become very slurred.

"You are the proof," said Mrs. Weekes, and hugged him harder.

"I have the proof of love," said Bobsy Marshall advancing.

"The proof of the pudding," said Domingo.

"Proof positive. Of hope for an unmolested future for the written word," said the J. P.

"At least 80 per cent proof," said Pimlott.

"Proofs are a thing of the past," said Sturridge.

"They always publish without proof," said Frank Wheeler.

"Prove it," said Joan.

"I hate poofs," said the mayor.

"I'm pissed," said Harris.

Now Boychester had shaken himself free of Mrs. Weekes, and in a sudden outbreak of conscientiousness, or was it just conscience or plain fear, was lurching through the door, across the foyer and into the street that would take him back round to the works. Domingo would have barred his exit except that he was locked in a violent struggle with Frank Wheeler. He had pulled the suede coat by the tail over the PR man's head and was dragging it towards the cloakroom with Wheeler's long ribby body wobbling blindly behind. Even Joan was laughing. Boychester slipped unsteadily past the pair and out onto the pavement. He had got about 20 yards when he heard the restaurant door open again and glanced round to see Mrs. Weekes and the squatter shape of Bobsy Marshall clattering neck and neck towards him. Were his eyes deceiving him, or were the two really swiping at each other with their handbags, like charioteers in a Roman epic?

He tried to accelerate, but the disappointing thighs didn't respond; the promptings of the brain were weak with alcohol. If anything, the women had the edge on him. The door opened yet a third time, and when Boychester looked, he could see, behind his pursuers, Domingo reversing out on to the pavement, still shouting and pulling at Frank Wheeler's coat. Frank was not yet fully parted from it, and his head was invisible. But the body was now in plain view, bent forward at a right angle like a giraffe in deep famine. After them the mayor came tumbling out, then the waitress, then Harris, until the pavement was full. Boychester ran on, as much to escape as to go and do the duties of his station.

If only he could have seen a certain profile through the window of his office, and the shadows it was casting on his ceiling, and the Jew who was taking his name and rifling his autonomy, he might have found an extra yard of pace.

Camina was not enjoying his work. That same feeling of nausea at being near to Boychester's soul, wrapped in his landscape, the feeling he had experienced the previous evening when walking through Brondesbury, was with him again. Here was the desk diary with its spongy red cover and its pages full of Buyers' promise. Here was the long plastic ruler which he would swish in the air as he lolled backwards on his chair. Here was the council yearbook, the Rotary calendar and the piece of paper with the guests from whom he was this very minute trying to flee. The smell of the man – an orange smell, that was the only word for it – was everywhere. Camina could not have felt the odious presence more strongly if he had been wearing Boychester's suit, driving his car, cradling his child.

But here also was the proof, pinned down like Gulliver. The last amendments had taken no time. Under the large photo were written the words: "Please substitute Caption B," and right across the bold type of the Message was the instruction: "Reset Roman."

The inefficiency potential of this was high. Camina considered the chances of this resetting coming unscathed through the last digestive heaves of the metal beast. Such type-setters as were around tonight would almost certainly be in the pub. There might be nobody in the proof-readers' room – not just for a single page. Certainly the head printer would cuss as never before at the late editorial whim which would put him back half an hour. Just as certainly, he would not put himself out one jot just to bail out the missing editor if there should be any . . . irregularities. Yes, thought Camina. The chances were bad, or rather, good.

There were footsteps in the corridor beyond the newsroom, two pairs of them, one shuffling, the other sharp. There was an exchange of abuse between the night-watchman and the printer. After a short silence there was more growling, like a dog catching a fox at the dustbin after dark, then the noise of a bottle smashing on the floor. Camina was astride the window ledge, swinging the right leg over, looking down at the drop, sitting on his hands, lowering himself forward into the dark.

As he picked himself up from the flower bed he could hear the door into Boychester's room click open. He stood up, flat against the wall. The footsteps tapped in above him. There was a rustling of paper as the printer grabbed the proof from the desk, then a soft, anguished "Oh, fucking hell."

"Matter, mere matter," said Camina to himself, remembering the Boychester line on printers. What was it he had said on the question of their concern for the subject matter of the type they handled? That they couldn't care less what the type said, just so long as it filled the paper and was on the stone in good time; that they only ever balked at references to their own intransigence. For the first time Camina hoped – how he hoped – that his boss had got it right.

The footsteps tapped out again. "Mere matter," Camina repeated. "They are blind to all meaning. Indeed, many would argue that this is the way it should be. I count myself as one of their number."

"Another fuck-up, Roy," said the printer as he reached the stone, still holding the proof. "Got a reset here and a new caption. Quick as you like, mate, and sod the readers' room. We'll bung it through unread. Fucked if I'm going to sod about here all night when there's no-one in editorial. Their funeral."

Roy took the proof, let out his own identical "Oh fucking hell," and headed for the linotype area calling "Norman!"

A few minutes later a solitary car in the old regatta was rising and falling in its own time. At the keys Norman lounged back in his chair, knees apart, like a lorry driver on a slow gradient. Beside the keyboard was the marked proof, and between these two points he swivelled his eyes as the machine tapped and clattered. From time to time he sang a snatch of song in a huge bellow which rang around the empty area and died away at the far end of the building.

The slugs fell in a row down the chute beside the keys. Twenty minutes later they were being slotted into place on the stone, from where the metal tray was then whisked away on a trolley for moulding. First the papier-mâché impression, the flong, and then the saddle-shaped slab of metal. Down to the rotary press it went, to be clamped round half a cylinder. The familiar rumble, as from a ship's engine, started and the broad band of paper began its course through the machine. As the rumble climbed to a roar, so the blur of black and white moved faster by, with the picture on the front page now forming its own elongated streak of grey. Very soon the first copies of the paper were plopping down rhythmically at the other end and being trundled down the belt of rollers into the loading bay where a van was waiting.

Upstairs in Boychester's office the head printer had ritually left a proof of the revised front page. The man who might have perused it was by now back in Domingo's, dragged there by the two women who had outrun him. The captain was absent from his bridge and on his desk was the most damning evidence of his dereliction. The crime of Helmut Boychester, 60, the flasher fined £40, was beyond rescinding. The whole building throbbed with the multiplying proof.

By the time the surly young messenger had appeared at the works, picked up a handful of copies from the belt and slouched off to find Mr. Boychester at Domingo's, the print run was almost finished, and the van half loaded with bundles. He shouldered his way through the door of the restaurant and was astounded by the noise. They were all still there: the mayor, Harris, Wheeler and Joan, the magistrate and her husband – everyone. The P.A. system was wound up to such a volume that the bass waves physically hit the messenger in the stomach.

In both hands he raised his bundle to shoulder height and shouted at the top of his voice: "Mr. Boy-chester!" All he could hear was the rattling of his own throat. He shouted again: "Bu-gle. Bew-gul!" Then he dropped the bundle on the floor with an unheard thud and glared into the human thicket that was shaking in front of him. As no-one took any notice he shrugged his shoulders and barged out into the street again.

The bundle lay there undiscovered against the wall for half an hour or more as the ankles teemed around it. Not until Harris tripped headlong over it on his way for some fresh air did it make itself known.

"Ha ha ha. Harris has gone down!" said the mayor. "I say. Hey. Everybody. Harris is taking the long count. One-a two-a three-a. Ha ha. Too much Britvic, eh? Ha ha!"

As he leaned over, he saw the title-piece on the top copy sticking out from under the knees of the fallen chauffeur. There was the sharp impression of the *Bugle*'s masthead, with its Old English script.

"I say! Everybody!" he bellowed again. "Listen, Domingo. Turn that din off. It's here."

"What is here?" asked the J. P.

"Hear hear," said the husband.

"The bloody Whatsit," said the mayor. "You know, what we're here for. The bloody *Bugle* thingy."

With the music off and the mayor bellowing, and the sight of Harris full length on the floor, a semi-circle of onlookers had formed around the spectacle. The mayor was tearing at the knot in the nylon string that was holding the bundle together.

"Gerroff Harris!" he shouted, and dragged the legs roughly to one side. He fumbled for a few seconds, before giving up and tugging the string down one side of the bundle. The loop slipped off and the mayor took up the top copy.

"Here we are then, ladies and gents," he said, with his best civic vowels. "An 'istoric moment is upon us. I have in my hands here a local document which is nothing more nor less than a collector's item."

He cleared his throat like an M. C. and tottered slightly. By now the semi-circle was packed tight and the empty restaurant floor behind could be seen littered with debris of every kind: cigarette ash, rice, mangled flowers, flattened canapés, whole chicken bones. Boychester was at the back of the group, flanked by Bobsy Marshall and Mrs. Weekes. He was pale and blinking, and as near to looking drawn as the round face would allow. But he brightened again and summoned the old smug set of the features as the mayor repeated "a collector's item" and expansively held the first of the last metal *Bugles* at arm's length in front of him.

Then, quite suddenly, the dignity and the sense of occasion on his face disappeared. In their place arrived the mirth of sheer disbelief. It started in the middle, at the mouth, and rippled its way out across the cheeks until the whole of the big face was shaking. Then there was a helpless wheezing noise and tears were starting from his eyes. He drew the paper back into his belly and hinged forward in pain. When he straightened up again he managed to blurt: "Brrrilliant . . . oh, dear Lord, it's bloody brrrilliant. Oh, ow, ow!"

Joan and the J. P. were bending down to pluck two more copies from under Harris's knees, but the mayor clamped one foot on the bundle. "No, no, no!" he shouted. "I've got to read it to you. Oh yes . . . Boychester. Yer best bleeding *Bugle* ever. Blooming brilliant. Listen to this. Here we go."

After another gale of laughter and more puzzled looks in

the audience, most of all between Boychester and Mrs. Weekes, he started again: "Here we go then . . . 'Editor Fined £40 for Gross Indecency.' " After the first paragraph he broke down again in the sentence beginning "Helmut Boychester, 60, of Boychester Towers, Brondesbury . . ." He tried to get restarted, but all in vain. Each time he came to the words "Boychester Towers, Brondesbury," another bout of wheezing started.

"I see," said the J. P. "It's a sort of spoof."

"That's right, love," said the mayor. "That's just what it is. Lovely stuff."

"A parody, what?" her husband chipped in.

"The very thing, Guv'nor," said the mayor.

"Well I do wish you'd let us all share the joke," said Joan. She stamped forward and tore a copy from under the mayor's foot. He recoiled into the corner with another silent intake of air for the next wheeze.

Suddenly all the copies in the pile had been pecked away like the canapés and were rustling white in the throng. Ffitch had one. So did the little councillor. So too the J. P. and her husband. And Domingo. Bobsy Marshall and Mrs. Weekes were clawing their way through from the back, craning over shoulders like very nosy neighbours at the fence.

"Super wheeze," said Ffitch, reading his copy. "I say, Boychester, you do have the whackiest sense of humour."

"Your work?" asked the J. P.'s husband in Boychester's direction. "Dashed funny. I do love a good spoof."

"That was the Irishman's case," said the J. P. reading on down the report.

"What case is that, dear?"

"This one here. The £40 fine. I was on the bench that morning. Yes, look. Here I am, mentioned – there. Oh, I see. Boychester's put his own name in. Yes, quite funny." There was a quizzical note.

"Probably the printers' little joke, dear," said the husband. "They do this sort of thing from time to time. Dummy, I think they call it."

"Odd sense of humour though," said the J. P.

"Oh, quite. Quite. Odd people."

"Good fun," said Ffitch. "Now, where's the real one?"

His eye had wandered into the middle of the reset Message to Our Readers, which now read like this: "For well over a century now the *Bugle* has brought you all the Bugel has borught you all the Blueg has Bungle Bungle Bungle broug you all news that is pri*!½ to squixrrr. We have boldly trodden the krodden the xrodde the grodden prodden mmmmmroddden wrodden the path pallthx of objuyektif xexcellenxce thrrrrreexcellence arrrreeeuuuo¾!** forelock touching ka chukka chikka fukka fukka fukka hexposed himself to two nuns.

"We have in short been your paper scrapyr xraper rtaper yaper change for the bllrrrghhrrr and rammed it between the uprights. Xprit plaxe yeru orderr xorder kxorderx now . . ." And so on to the end in a bewildering torrent of transposed lines, refugees from other stories, and sheer gibberish. A more convincing message on the need for a new and efficient technology couldn't have been scripted.

Beneath the picture of Sturridge and Hubbard with the freshly installed machinery in Holborn was this caption: "Butch and Sundance plot their next move in a tense scene from the Newman/Redford classic at the Gaumont."

Mrs. Weekes had fought her way to the front of the throng ahead of Bobsy Marshall and had read round the corner of Ffitch's elbow.

"He's such a witty one," she said. "It's probably his work, but he's just kept it quiet to surprise us."

Ffitch and a few others were now in the same state as the mayor.

"Of course, it could have been the printers," Mrs. Weekes went on. "He's a great favourite of theirs. They occasionally do this sort of thing on special occasions for the people they like."

"Better than the real thing," yelped the tiny councillor.

"Some of your lot don't make any more sense than that in council meetings," bellowed the mayor.

As Boychester's witty work made its impact there was just for a second – and it was not long enough to leave a lasting impression – a pricking of doubt in certain heads. It was brought on by the harmless remark of the J. P.'s husband: "Well you know, papers really do drop clangers like this from time to time. They have actually gone on the streets in this state. Jolly funny, but terrible really."

So was this an inspired parody of the old technology? If it was not Boychester's work, surely it was too subtle to have been done by the printers. Two people, one dead and the other absent, would have known that such banana skin humour was not the editor's hallmark. Why were all these guests laughing so riotously at a joke made by the paper, apparently against the paper, with a Readers' Message in pure Martian and a huge report of the flashing editor's court case written by his own reporter?

The doubt didn't take root. It was simply Boychester being brilliant. How shabby to think otherwise. Besides, the J. P. was turning round to the group at her back and declaiming: "We shall have the truth from the author himself. Where is the clever fellow? Boychester!"

More voices took up the cry until it sounded like a whole courtroom baying for a defendant to be brought up from the cells. The J. P. wished for a gavel but had to make do with a "Ssssh!"

In the lull that followed the last calls for the hour's hero it dawned on everyone there that Boychester was no longer present. All the heads had turned to follow the lead of the J. P.; and now they all stared not at the man who would naturally have found himself centre-stage in their vision, but across the empty foyer to the door marked "Gentlemen."

There were those who swore – and still do to this day – that Boychester made his getaway through the lavatory window, and those who said that it wasn't nearly wide enough. Domingo himself was adamant that no-one had passed by through the glass door at the front. The J. P. would gladly have chaired an inquiry on the incident. She still would.

Whatever the truth, Boychester was at that moment half way to the works as fast as he could go, perhaps faster, leaving Ffitch and the rest waiting in the restaurant for the very thing they already had, while he was wondering whether that glimpsed mutation of a front page could be believed.

It was three o'clock. On any Friday morning at this time Boychester would have been snoring heavily next to Mrs. B., with one of her tremendous arms draped lovingly across him. If she had been woken by a child she would have been lying there staring with worship into her husband's face and blessing her great fortune. Another triumphant week would have been over and the Buyers' liquor of the evening would have been working slowly through Boychester's prone hulk.

But not tonight. As he padded heavily round into Fountain Street he had time to reflect for a second on all the industry – the machinery, the noise, the men moving about in the works and shouting to each other, the bright lights, the bare bulbs, the smell of paper and hot oil, the bundles being rolled out and thrown into the van – which pumped his *Bugle* through into the public consciousness long after his own work was done.

By now all this had stopped. The huge doors at the mouth of the loading bay were closed and the entire building was blind and deaf. The vehicle that was disappearing round the corner at the end of the road: could that have been the van setting off on its round of the newsagents?

Panting and gasping in this nightmare, he came level with the railings over which Camina had climbed five hours earlier. There was the single lit window of his office throwing its square of light across the garden below. As Boychester looked up at it the shadow of the nightwatchman moved on the wall and the light went off. The entire building was dark. Boychester felt himself on a railway platform surrounded by the familiar streets of his home town, but the whole lot suddenly transported into the middle of nowhere, a landscape of dark canyons and unscalable cliffs. Only the track threaded its way safely through, but the last train was gone and there would never be another one. Never ever. The buildings were cardboard façades mocking him with the illusion of friendliness. All the rail staff had gone home for good; the destination boards were bolted up into their pillar, with only half a place name visible to show the stranded passenger where he should now be. Boychester also imagined he saw two men of different ages dismantling the track with crowbars.

It was raining again. In the empty street he yelled: "I am Boychester! Boyyyy-chester!" as loud as the messenger. "I am Boychester of the Bew-Gul!"

"Your kingdom for a horse, eh?" said a voice behind him. "Ha ha, well I never. Not THE Mr. Boychester. Why, yes it is. Remember you well."

Boychester turned sharply on his heels, and the man facing him said: "I am on the marketing side these days. Yes. A consultancy post with a major concern. Well, well."

It was Sizer, the old Sizer of the ashtray and the sugar basin. He was wearing the cotton jacket, and the eyes stared out vacantly through the glasses below his institutional haircut.

"Well out of it. Well well out of it. Oh dear me yes. Still there, are you, I expect. Ah well."

Boychester drew back a pace and then advanced again to grip the man by the lapels. "The list," he yelled. "You must give me the list. You must have one on you."

"A list?" said Sizer. "No, no. Afraid I can't help you at all."

"Of the newsagents," cried Boychester. "For Christ's sake, you know what I mean, man. The delivery run. Where the van goes."

Sizer looked utterly lost. Very slowly, and with his head cocked compassionately on one side, he said: "What appears to be the matter? Is something wrong?"

Boychester had taken out his wallet and was tearing from it every pound note it contained. He grabbed Sizer's hand and closed the fist round the money. Then he delved deep into the wallet again for any change. A shower of coins fell on to the pavement, so too did three or four credit cards.

covering at least ten miles in the two hours that remained before the newsagents would come down to take in their stock. It could have been then he wondered about the completeness of the list, or again when he remembered the hundreds of copies sent out on subscription. Not even Freedom's Friend could snare his own untruth in a butterfly net.

At some point he did go into a phone box and call a mini-cab. (The driver reported the incident to the police the following day and then told the story in the Chairmen.) When the cab arrived Boychester was standing on the pavement with three or four more bundles. The driver, who was offered a vast fee and, like Sizer, any written undertaking, was to help load these into the car and then drive to a cul-de-sac that ran to the edge of the Grand Union Canal. The driver refused, or so he claimed. However, a few days later one of the reps from Holborn did discover the soaking shreds of what must have been many copies, while walking on the towpath.

Elsewhere in the borough a night shift worker on his way home saw two bundles blazing on an empty plot near his house. Boychester's random route took him back to a road near Domingo's, where he saw a Rolls parked diagonally on a crossroads. All four doors were open, the radio was blaring, and Harris was spilled out from the driver's seat with his top half on the road. In the back was the nearly naked waitress, and the mayor was climbing out to pour his chauffeur back into the car. He was bellowing "Love all this" and Boychester hurried off again.

During these small but growing hours he must have seen much that was new to him: a lone juggernaut pounding across the city, with its brakes hissing monstrously on an empty bend; a butcher setting off to market in his estate car with a metal tray in the back; the first milk float; the first bus, empty; a cold streaky sky beginning to light above the gasometer; the sound of a farming programme coming clearly from a front room; birds twittering in the small parks; individual motors merging into a wider drone; all the symptoms of an outbreak of day.

He also passed his own home and Larch Towers, facing each other blamelessly across the street; and The Trenches, although he didn't know it, where Camina slept free of dreams above an empty room with undrawn curtains.

By the end of the night, by the time that day was a clinical reality, Boychester no longer looked for bundles. A newsagent in a dowdy little parade could be seen laying out the *Bugles* at the front of his counter. The first customer, a toothless old woman in a baggy coat, with two tiny dogs panting on their leads, came out with a packet of cigarettes and a copy of the paper.

Soon the streets were filling with people. Freedom's Friend was one of many, rubbing shoulders with the early risers. Some looked well slept and purposeful. In a larger street nearer the High Road he was passed by a man who left a scent of aftershave in his wake. Two young brothers in cadets' uniforms came out of a gate carrying kit bags and checking their rail passes. Only Boychester had all his destinations behind him.

Four miles away in the sorting office were many different newspapers, all folded into their stickers. One was on its way to Weybridge for the perusal of some admiring parents-in-law, who also blessed their great fortune.

At about the same time as Hubbard, early as ever, saw his picture on the front page in the boardroom at Holborn, Mrs. Boychester in her dressing-gown opened the front door ajar and peered out into the street. There was worry and bewilderment in her face as she looked up and down the pavement. George loitered behind her. She was at the ready with the "Clever Boychy" that her husband was never to hear.